I0620808

FORGOTTEN PAGES

Denise Landry

Copyright © 2012 Denise Landry

ISBN-13: 978-0615640549

All rights reserved. No part of this publication may be reproduced, stored in a retrieval system, or transmitted in any form or by any means, electronic, mechanical, recording or otherwise, without the prior written permission of the author.

The characters and events in this book are fictitious. Any similarity to real persons, living or dead is purely coincidental and not intended by the author.

Printed in the United States of America.

This book is dedicated to my mother Jacque and my father Merle.
Thank you both for always being there for me.

Kay frantically ran toward the front door, just as she put her hand on the screen door to escape she was hit by overwhelming fear when hearing the sound of him yelling, "Stop!"

As she stood frozen in the doorway, she could smell whiskey wafting from every pore of his body as he sat on the couch just several feet behind her. Nauseated and paralyzed by the stench of alcohol and the harshness in his voice, she was unable to move or decide what to do. Should I open the door and run, or listen to the man? She backed away from the door and slowly turned around to look at him. She could never have imagined what would happen next and then she heard the piercing noise of the gun shot.

1

Suddenly, Kay was wide awake, in a cold sweat. She had been having the reoccurring nightmare off and on for over twenty five years. When stress got the best of her, the nightmare seemed to come more often, and for the last year it had been disturbing her sleep on a regular basis. This time, she blamed it on Arizona, where she would be the following day.

Pull it together, Kay, she scorned herself as she felt the dampness on the pillowcase. Lauren, her daughter, was taking a shower, and the last thing she wanted to do was to appear distraught in front of her. She grabbed a water bottle from the nightstand and began to guzzle it, used the bed sheet to wipe the perspiration from her forehead then glanced over at the digital alarm clock. It was already ten o'clock! She jumped out of bed and began packing for the noon flight.

Lauren came out of the bathroom and sat on the bed and watched as her mother organized her paperwork; that spread out all over the suite they had shared for over a week. There were stacks of folders in a rainbow of colors, and they were all related to her upcoming case in an Arizona courtroom. It amounted to over a year's worth of evidence, along with attorney notes and emails. It was all part of the deal: If she wanted to go to Scotland, she had to haul the forest worth of documents with her. Her attorney's wanted her prepared for the trial when she returned. As much as Lauren understood the importance of

6

the paperwork, the mess had been driving her crazy. She had always been organized and had learned to pack light over the years, unlike her mother.

In spite of the pre-courtroom drama, it was an exciting week for both of them. Kay was so happy she could get away to see her daughter play golf in the European tournament. Even though there wasn't much free time during their stay Kay took the evenings to read and reread the case files and felt she was prepared for what lie ahead.

Lauren started rambling on about her schedule for the next two months, as if her mother was going to remember all it by heart. Kay finished packing up her belongings she called for the bellhop. They walked down to the hotel lobby together, where Kay waited for a shuttle to take her to the airport.

With tears in her eyes, Lauren hugged her mother tightly and said, "I love you. Thanks for coming to watch me play."

Kay hugged her back, as if she never wanted to let her go. "I wouldn't have missed it for the world."

"I wish you could stay one more day and to think you could, if you had settled out of court instead of trying to fight this thing, it's frustrating." Kay burst into laughter and grabbed Lauren's hands. "It's not just about the money! It's about justice. I know you don't understand, but the whole thing will be over soon, I promise."
"I wish I could be there to support you in Phoenix, but, well, you know."

"Yes, I know, honey. You're a busy girl.

They embraced once more and finally let go, and with her eyes filling with tears, she turned and walked through the revolving doors to her waiting shuttle.

That evening, Lauren met up with some of the competitors she had met that week. They had dinner and drinks and discussed where they were headed next. Lauren kept it to herself that the following day, she was doing a

7

photo shoot for *Golf Digest*. There was too much competitive jealousy on the circuit, and she was a humble girl that loved to keep secrets.

* * *

Lauren had qualified for the LPGA in late August. By the end of October, she was playing in her first major tournament, which had taken her to Scotland. Sports writers had said she had "a natural swing" and was "dedicated to the game," so it was no surprise that in just a few short months, she was already ranked among the top ten female golfers in the world. Placing fourth on the European tour and winning a fifty thousand dollar purse was a stellar achievement for young Lauren, and no one could blame her for being on cloud nine.

She was looking forward to returning home to Salt Lake City, but she had to stop off in New York for another tournament and a meeting with one of the editors for *Golf Digest* who was writing an article about her.

As a young golf prodigy, Lauren was getting a lot of attention now and being contacted by different sponsors. Not only could she play the game, but off the course, she was a natural beauty and very photogenic. She was a rarity: a beautiful American world-class golfer. Her piercing blue eyes and light brown hair, perfect jaw line, and ivory complexion made her stand out in an industry saturated with Asian competitors.

Kay had never been much of a golfer, but she enjoyed watching Lauren play. Lauren was a real crowd pleaser and had energy and a calmness about her that kept people enthralled during the tours and intrigued with her life outside the competition.

Golf and Kay didn't mesh well because unlike her daughter, she didn't have the patience to exceed in such a slow, methodical sport.

Kay had lived a hard life. Over the past year, it had really started to show. Her once-piercing green eyes had grown increasingly hollow, and she looked as worn out as she was. She had always considered herself strong and resilient, but that resilience seemed to be failing her. She was in the middle of a major battle and looking for closure and justice.

They had finally reached some smooth sailing after years of ups and downs and a tumultuous mother/daughter relationship. They always had a hard time understanding each other. They were complete opposites, Lauren knew her mother loved her, but they were never on the same page—rarely even in the same book, truth be told.

Lauren's golf career would now place her as part of the jet set. Unlike in her growing-up years, though, she'd be moving around by her own choice and not because of forces beyond her control.

Lauren had attended Penn State on a full-ride golf scholarship, but after two years, she quit school and signed up to qualify for the LPGA. Birdies and pars were more important to her than textbooks and mortarboards. Kay was disappointed when she heard that her daughter had quit school, but she was never allowed to have much to say in what Lauren wanted to do with her life. Lauren had always been stubborn and was focused on one thing her goal of finally becoming a professional golfer.

When Lauren reached that level in her sport, her mother knew she would be globe-trotting. Kay planned to spend time with her whenever she could. If Kay wasn't required to be in Phoenix for the court date, she would have stayed the extra day in Scotland and proudly accompanied her daughter to the photo shoot. She hated that she had to leave her daughter's side, and even more troubled that she had to go back Arizona, a state she had come to hate. *But that's what happens when you're the lead plaintiff in a monumental trial,* she told herself.

* * *

Lauren's photo shoot the next morning was a relatively painless process. The magazine was thrilled with her pictures and could not wait to put her on the cover of their upcoming edition. Lauren hated posing for the cameras but loved the accolades she received.

After her photo shoot, she returned to the hotel room and started packing up her belongings. As she gave the room the once-over to be sure she wasn't leaving anything behind, she noticed something dark in between the bed and nightstand. Her mother had left something: a dark brown accordion folder file, so dark that it took a minute for Lauren to realize what it was. Inside the file were several envelopes and a thick notebook, along with paperwork. Lauren was annoyed at her mother's sloppy carelessness, especially since now she'd have to make room for the file in her carry-on. Her anxiousness to get to the airport and start the long journey back to America only made her more irritable about little hassles like this.

Once she arrived at the airport and began to board the plane, she realized she had gotten lucky: The plane was only at half-capacity, and she had three empty seats to herself. As the plane took off, she sat looking out the window at Glasgow; there was a sigh of relief. She knew she had done well and was proud of her own accomplishments.

She had many hours of travel ahead of her, which included one stopover in London before she would arrive in New York City. As she settled into her seat, it hit her that she had been running nonstop for over a week and needed to sleep. She reached into her brown leather carry-on bag to get out her iPod, which was buried under her mother's forgotten file. She pulled out file and grabbed her iPod, but as she began to stuff the file back into the bag, curiosity got the best of her, and she decided to take a closer look. She wondered what her mother had left behind. She opened the accordion folder and looked over some of the documents, mainly emails between Kay and her attorney. She then pulled out the notebook which read

10

"Dr. Henderson/Personal." *Not anymore,* Lauren thought, laughing. She had no idea that what she was about to read was no laughing matter.

She was intrigued and wondered if her mother had realized what she had left behind. If so, she knew she'd have a voicemail from her mother about it by the time she landed in New York.

As her flight took to the sky, Lauren flipped open the notebook and began reading. Little did she know that as the plane thrust forward, she'd be journeying into the past.

2

People were yelling and screaming, but Kay just wanted to sleep. She was having a wonderful dream. She was in the middle of free falling, her stomach full of butterflies as she sat in the front seat of the rollercoaster. The red metal tracks were spread out in front of her, and she could hear the *click-clack* as the coaster moved along it was just about to drop down another steep hill when she was shaken awake by someone yelling, "Wake up!" *Can't I just sleep?* She thought, slipping stubbornly into consciousness. *Why did they have to ruin the perfect ride?*

She was only able to barely open her eyes and see a hazy sheet of broken glass. It was shaped like a spider web. It was the windshield she had been tossed into, head first, just several minutes earlier. As her senses awoke, she smelled gas and felt hot air on her face. Then she remembered being pulled from the car and carried to the side of the road and placed next to her friend, who was bleeding and unconscious like she had been just moments earlier. People kept telling Kay and her friend to stay awake. Kay opened her eyes again to see a woman running around, franticly begging for water. She started to fall asleep again and suddenly felt the warmth of water being poured over her face. She lifted her hands to wipe the water out of her eyes, but when she pulled her hands down into her line of sight, she saw that it wasn't water at all, but bright red blood. The thick humidity and heat made it nearly impossible for Kay to stay conscious. She was lying on hot gray rocky pavement and it was extremely uncomfortable. "Stay with us," she heard over and over. "Stay awake." No matter how hard she tried, though, she could not hold on to her consciousness with the merciless sun beating down on her face and faded into a deep sleep.

This time, she dreamt of two men in white uniforms picking her up. She woke a final time to the doors of an ambulance being opened, and she told the two men who carried the fragile ten-year-old into the emergency room that they were in her dream. They looked at each other like she was crazy, and like Dorothy returning from Oz, she tried to convince them it was true.

Kay entered the emergency room, where her mother Suzanne and father John were waiting anxiously. The first thing her father said to Kay was, "You know, now when you get older and your boyfriend is driving fast, you can tell him to slow down because you were in a car accident."

That's strange, Kay thought to herself.

"Thank goodness!" her mother said, looking at her face. "We thought you had had your teeth knocked out."

Right about then her Uncle Hugh, her father's brother, walked into the room and started yelling at Kay. "Why didn't you give the police our phone number? How could you be so stupid? Ricky was in that car with you, and we needed to know! God, Kay, you are such a dumb ass sometimes!"

Ricky, six years old at the time, and was Hugh's son. He was in the back seat of the car when it was struck by the drunk driver. Small as he was, Ricky came out of the accident without a scratch, but as always Hugh couldn't have cared less about Kay or anyone besides himself. He did not even notice that her head and knees were bandaged and bleeding, and he wasn't concerned at all about his niece's wellbeing. He had no idea she had been unconscious most of the last hour, not that it would have made any difference to him.

Kay knew Hugh was a mean man, and she was used to being talked down to by him. In the midst of her confusion and pain, there was one brief moment when the world seemed to stop and she went into a state of complete shock.

Her father John started yelling loudly at his brother. "Hugh, get the hell out of here! Can't you see she is hurt?"

13

Kay had heard her father yell many times before, but never on her behalf; always seemed to be just the opposite. Was she imaging it, or maybe the medication they'd given her had knocked her a bit loopy. She would have thought she'd be scolded for upsetting him, but instead her father stood up for her. She was even more surprised when her father demanded that she be taken to a private room where her and her friend Janie could stay under the doctors' care until released.

Janie's mother had been driving the car they were in, taking Kay and the other kids on a swimming outing, which would have been a nice relief from the torturous heat. They were just two miles from the community pool, when a truck driven by a drunk driver hit the yellow hatchback.

Kay had been sitting in the front seat in the middle right near the manual shift. Janie was next to her and closest to the passenger window. When the truck collided with the little car, Kay was thrown head first into the windshield, and her knees were instantly bloodied from being smashed against the dash. Painful as it was, it was that dash that saved her life. Seatbelts were not mandatory in the late 1970's, and airbags were still stuff in Sci-Fi movies.

Janie, thirteen, had sustained plenty of her own injuries. Her head and face were now wrapped with white gauze, and she was not coherent. Kay had heard the doctors talking saying she may have a fractured skull, but it was still too early to tell for sure. She had hit the windshield and then the passenger side window with the side of her face and head. Kay overheard the doctors saying Janie would have to have reconstructive surgery on her face once she was better.

After only a couple of days Kay was released from the hospital. A week later, Janie's condition deteriorated, she ended up passing away from a brain hemorrhage due to her fractured skull. When Kay heard the news, she was traumatized. She felt guilty, like she'd somehow used her

14

friend for a shield to save her own life. *What if I had traded places with Janie instead of sitting in the middle next to her mother?* She was overcome with guilt and grief, and she could not fathom that she would never see Janie again. They had spent hours riding their bikes, playing games and swimming, they were best friends. It was hard for Kay to comprehend that it had all come to an abrupt end, and in such a tragic way. Her parents never spoke about Janie's death or the accident, acting as though it never happened at all. Needless to say, there was never any counseling. The only proof Kay had that she was in the accident and lost a friend to a careless drunk driver were the tiny scars that were left on her forehead and knees. But there were also deep scars that lingered in her memory.

Lauren was caught off guard and wondered what in the hell she was reading. Is this really about my mother? Did she...God, did she write all of this? I had no idea...

Her mother had never once mentioned the accident to her. She looked down at the pages and thumbed through them again, wondering if it was all fiction or if, in fact, she was reading about her mother's life. Like a novel she couldn't put down, she kept reading as the plane ripped through the blue sky splitting the clouds.

3

It had been only a couple of months since the accident and Janie's passing. As she sat on the floor coloring a rainbow in all the wrong colors, she overheard her parents discussing the possibility of moving. Since Suzanne and John took little time to explain anything to their kids, Kay and Luke, Kay dismissed their talk of Utah as something she should not concern herself with and continued coloring the third stripe a dismal shade of gray.

At the time, they lived in Orville, a very rural one-light town in northeastern Ohio. They owned a small three-bedroom ranch-style home that sat on five acres of wooded area. Her whole family, including thirteen cousins and both of her grandmothers, lived within several miles of each other. Kay had only left the area a few times. Having spent her eleven years in such a small world, a kind of bubble-enclosed existence, moving away was not something Kay could fully comprehend. All she knew about Utah was that it had large mountains; something she had never seen and had only read about in fairytales and had to mark on maps she made for school.

Kay was a scrawny little girl with skin so white it looked as if she had never seen the sun. She had very fine dark hair and green eyes. Her hair would curl during the hot, humid Ohio summers. She always dressed in clothing her mother made for her and/or hand-me-downs that her thirteen cousins were kind enough to pass on.

Her father was not at all complimentary about Kay's appearance. He often made rude comments and told Kay in no uncertain terms how unattractive she was, going so far as to banish her from his sight. He seemed to be particularly bothered by her permanent teeth when they grew in, they were bucked and he thought it made her look terribly homely. "You are so ugly I can't even look at you," he often said to his daughter. Then he would turn to

Suzanne, Kay's mother, and demand, "Get her out of my face. I can't look at her." Even though his constant tirades and insults hurt Kay immensely as she was growing up, by age eleven she had become numb to it.

Kay was a daydreamer. She had to be to escape the reality that swallowed her. She dreamt of big, faraway places and often pondered what it would be like to see them. She dreamt of the perfect home, and she added imaginary things to that imaginary home each day. This included children of her own, two boys and two girls. The girls shared a pink room and the boys a blue one. Many hours went into building her imaginary domicile, and once it was built, she spent most of her time there in that perfectly peaceful place where everything was beautiful and everyone got along and no one told anyone else how ugly they were. She created her dream home with ideas she gleaned from some of the beautiful houses she admired near where she lived. There was a certain white house with pillars and black shutters; that house captured her attention and served as the canvas on which she painted her dreams. She often rode her Blue Streak banana seat bike around the small town, pretending it was a sports car. She had turn blinkers under her banana seat, and the basket on her U-shaped handlebars made for a perfect pretend dash. She dreamt up anything and everything that would help her escape the real world.

Since her first grade year, Kay had had a crush on a blond-haired, blue-eyed boy named Teddy. They were both in fourth grade by this time, and even though he still thought girls had cooties and obviously had no interest in Kay, she had conjured up a whole life with him. In her dreams, she was Mrs. Teddy Knight-in-Shining-Armor, and she shared her life in that perfect house along with their four children with him, never a worry in the world.

Kay's last name was Whitley, so it was easy enough for kids to tease her based solely on that if nothing else. The boys at school, literary geniuses that they were, realized her name rhymed with "Shitley" and called her that until she cried, giving them all the more reason to tease her further.

In spite of all the teasing and her failed efforts to fit in with the boys, Kay was able to maintain straight A's. She had made several friends that she bonded with over schoolwork, but for the most part, she had gotten used to a solitary life. She spent hours alone, sometimes just lying in the grass of her large front lawn, looking up in the sky. She watched the white lines left in the wake of the planes flying thirty thousand feet overhead; she wondered where they were going and if she would ever get to go there someday. When she heard her father's truck coming up the rock driveway to her home, she knew the best way to escape his daily drama was to run off into the woods behind her home to play in her more beautiful, safer, happier imaginary world.

John was a heavy drinker and a huge bully. He was a burly man who was always pissed off about something— a real rugged man's man, who couldn't remember anything except being in the Marines. He spent most of his time after work with his drinking buddies at the American Legion. Other spare time was spent hunting, fishing or carousing with other woman. He was miserable at home, and he didn't bother trying to hide it.

His being gone most of the time was just fine with Kay and the rest of the family, except for Suzanne, Kay's mother. It wasn't that she missed her husband out of love and a yearning to be with him, but she wanted him home so she could save face with the neighbors. Suzanne was a beautiful brunette with brown eyes and fair skin. She always wanted everything to be perfect, and since it wasn't, she became an expert at making it look that way. She was a pleaser when it came to John and would do anything to get him to spend time at home, just so it would look like they were one big happy family.

She was very concerned that somebody might find out that John did not come home at night or that he was sleeping with any woman—or women. Everyone already

19

knew the truth, but they didn't have the heart to break it to her that her secrets were not secrets at all. Suzanne spent hours upon hours cleaning, painting, and wall papering—anything to make the house more of a home—in hopes that she could make the place so wonderful that John would want to spend more time there. Once, she painted the entire outside of their home, which was no easy task. When John got back from a hunting trip he had supposedly been on, he actually had the gall to complain, "Suzanne, why didn't you paint the inside too?"

Almost everyone was frightened and intimidated by John. He had a temper that only got worse when fueled by the bottle, and just like Kay herself, her aunts, uncles, and cousins were always on pins and needles when he was around. The only person who wasn't afraid of John was Luke, Kay's little brother. John seemed to tolerate Luke better than most, and vice versa. The boy had dark curly hair and hazel eyes just like Kay's. He was very quiet, but all boy.

Luke saw his father mistreat Kay, but he kept to himself and played. He knew his sister did her best to stay out of range of their angry father, and if she didn't, the monster would literally pick her up throw her out of the way. Luke, only two years younger than his sister, was torn. He loved and trusted his father but also loved his sister. He knew better, though, than to let his father see that they got along. When John was around, Luke intentionally picked fights with Kay; he had to prove to his dad that he could be just like him.

Kay spent most of her time at her cousins' homes, even though it was very rare for them to come visit her home. She felt out of place at her girlfriends' homes. When their fathers would come home and hug the kids or eat dinner with them, it was very uncomfortable for her. On the rare occasions that she did eat dinner with her own father, he was quick to ruin it.

He seemed to flip out over the smallest things, and once he beat Kay for not drinking her milk. He had the kind of temper that kept everyone on edge, never knowing what would happen next. Once, Kay faced his violent wrath just because she fidgeted with the pack of cigarettes on the dashboard of his old pickup truck. She did not think it would affect him, but it did everything affected John. His words seemed to be more hurtful than his belt, stick, hand, or whatever it was he used to induce pain. His words cut deeper than a knife.

Her mother Suzanne, who worshipped John, had high hopes that moving the family to Utah would change things. She convinced herself that if she could just get John away from his trouble-making alcoholic buddies, then maybe her alcoholic abusive husband would turn into a prince. Maybe he would happily stay home and become a family man. Suzanne had Catholic roots and her family did not believe in divorce, even though she had converted from Catholic to a devout Christian. She was not about to give up on the dream of having a perfect family. She hoped and prayed daily that things would get better. Kay wasn't the only one living in a dreamland.

Kay had visions of what Utah would be like and assumed if her family was going to move, it was going to be by plane. She and envisioned a large moving truck pulling up in front of their house to take all their belongings. Little did Kay know her father had a different plan.

One afternoon after Kay had finished playing with her cousins she was headed home on her bike. As she got closer to her home she could see something in the front yard. It was a huge old 1966 Bluebird school bus, painted a god-awful shade of dark brown with the words "Church of Christ" stenciled crudely on the side. Her brother and his friend were playing in it. Kay threw down her bike and ran inside, where she found her mother on the phone in tears. "What's the bus in the yard for?" she asked.

"That is what he is moving us in," Suzanne sobbed.

What? Kay thought. *Wait a minute...what about my first airplane ride and the big moving truck?*

In shock, Kay ran outside where Luke and a lot of the neighbor kids were playing in the bus. When her father came home, she said the one thing John did not want to hear. "I thought a big truck would come to move our stuff while we flew on a plane."

He immediately yelled, "We don't have that kind of fucking money! Now get your ugly ass out of my face and go play." Again, there was never any explanation. Kay and Luke just had to watch what was happening from the sidelines.

* * *

Over the next several weeks, Kay watched as her father ripped out and hauled away thirty-seven of the forty seats on the bus. He used brown paint to cover all the windows, minus the front four so the family could sightsee along the way. Apparently, the dark paint was to cover any evidence of their soon-to-be-loaded cargo. He also made sure to paint over the "Church of Christ" logo; he had no intention of looking like a family of missionaries. He was not really the religious sort. He had been raised Lutheran but had stopped attending church after returning from Vietnam.

Each day the house grew emptier. John and Suzanne sold every piece of furniture they did not need, but they kept the antiques that were given to them years earlier by the old lady who sold them their first home. Each piece was carefully placed and packed into the bus as so not to break during the long journey. Her father took one of the three bus seats that were left and turned it around so it faced another bus seat and placed their small kitchen table between them. It was a place for them to play games and or eat while John drove. He had packed the bus full, but still made sure there was enough room to live in during the long drive to Utah. It was going to be a long and slow trip because the bus was old, and John knew it was going to be no picnic hauling his wife and his two kids across the country to a place none of them had ever seen. John decided to make the trip more interesting by buying a CB radio so he could talk with truckers. Also, an avid hunter, he could not bear to leave all four of his coon dogs behind; he brought one along. He had one more surprise for the family when he invited his friend Bart to come along. Bart was an old drinking buddy who needed a lift out West. John agreed to lend him a hand and in return, Bart would help him drive the rickety old bus all the way to Utah.

Kay assumed they were going to Utah for a better life, maybe even a better job for her father, who had been laid off from a tire company a year earlier where he worked fixing conveyer belts. He had tried selling insurance in order to make a living, but it was clear he was not the salesman type. He did not have the personality or the communication skills to talk anyone into buying anything except maybe a beer at the local American Legion. Kay did not know her father's new job in Utah was for a meager four dollars and fifty cents an hour working in the rifle department of a sporting goods store.

They decided to leave at night after a long couple of days of teary-eyed goodbyes, minus one sad farewell to Uncle Hugh. They all loaded into the bus and said one final farewell to Kay's grandmother. Kay, in her tattered hand-me-down overall's clung to her grandma while sobbing. She did not want to let her go. It had finally hit her that she was really leaving the only home she had ever known, and there was no turning back. As she stepped onto the step of the bus, Kay looked back at the house and thought about running inside to hide, but the house was dark and empty. As her father cranked back the handle to open and close the old squeaky bus door, Luke and Kay began to cry. Kay couldn't help it. She knew nothing would ever be the same again.

"Shut the fuck up!" her father howled, and they all did the best they could to muffle their broken-hearted cries.

The bus was musty and felt unsteady as it rocked and bounced its way out of the yard; it had not been moved for over a month. It was pitch black out, and Kay did not understand why they had to leave in the middle of the night. She came to find out later that it was because Suzanne had begged John to leave when it was dark to avoid the embarrassment of a lasting picture of them leaving town in that terrible old bus.

The bus was so old they had to drive slowly. It took six hours just to cross the Ohio turnpike to enter Indiana. When the bus engine started to overheat and stall out, they had to wait for a tractor-trailer to tow them to a shop in Granger, Indiana. While the bus was being worked on, Kay and Luke played games they loved: Bingo or checkers. It kept them busy for hours and kept their minds off the fact they just left behind everything and everyone they had ever known.

There was not any money to be spent on a hotel and barely enough for food. They spent long hours, both days and nights, in the bus. On the third day, they finally headed into Illinois they were about fifty miles south of Chicago and it was around five o'clock in the evening when they hit rush-hour traffic. Kay's father was not a people person to begin with, and a traffic jam in an old bus was not something he was prepared for. In anger and frustration over taking a wrong exit heading north toward Chicago, John began cursing and yelling and searching for a place to pull over to let the traffic pass by.

Kay listened to her father go on and on in a tirade about how pissed off he was. She had never seen so many cars in her life. She had always heard of traffic jams, but now she was actually in one. It was so exciting to her, even in the middle her angry father's rant. He had done her a favor, and his frustrated detour would allow her to see a big city for the first time in her life. She was mesmerized by all the cars and trucks whizzing by. Through the massive sea of roadside trees, she saw that they were getting nearer and nearer to something large. *Chicago*, she thought, but it was really just a large hotel that bridged the massive freeway. For the first time, Kay witnessed a world that was so much more exciting than any she had ever known or even imagined.

Although it was thrilling to the wide-eyed Kay and Luke, the traffic jam was hell to her father as he kept the bus plugging along at a snail's pace. He was at his wits' end, trying to find a place to park until the traffic had subsided. Finally, he decided to take the exit for the hotel, and he parked the big old brown bus in the hotel parking lot.

When he opened the door of the bus to go and buy some sandwiches, he asked Kay and Luke to come help him. The traffic was louder than anything Kay had ever heard, the air was thicker than any Kay had ever breathed, and everything bigger than anything she had ever seen. As they walked into the hotel, it seemed as if everyone was staring at them. Luke and Kay looked like two little rag dolls. They stood in awe, for they had never seen anything as big and luxurious as that hotel in their entire lives. The ceiling seemed to be one hundred feet high and the lobby was decorated with giant potted plants and plush dark blue carpet imbedded with little white stars. It was an amazing sight to behold, and all the little country bumpkins could utter was "Wow!" over and over again.

John walked into the hotel deli, with his children in tow. They stood in line at a cafeteria-style counter. After their father ordered sandwiches and they continued to move through the line, their mouth-gaping awe was abruptly interrupted by John's loud holler at the cashier. "Are you fucking kidding me? Eighteen dollars just for some fucking sandwiches?"

Kay was shocked and wanted to leave, but he just kept on going. It felt to her like he would never shut up. Kay could see everyone looking at them with disbelief, and she could not wait to leave the hotel, but nothing prepared her for what she was about to witness when they walked outside.

25

As the automatic doors opened, Kay felt a sense of relief to escape the stares and people gawking at them. Then, when she saw the bus in the distance, her heart sank deep in her chest. She was mortified as she looked at a shirt her mother had washed in the restroom and hung out to dry on the side view mirror and at the big black hunting dog tied to the hinge of the bus. All of the excitement and thrill of seeing something new was ruined. Young as she was, she could sense that they didn't fit in and were a long way from home. She was overwhelmed with embarrassment. She climbed back onto the bus, laid down on one of the seats, closed her eyes and began to escape into one of her safe, beautiful and secret daydreams.

Lauren stopped reading when there was a slight jolt in her stomach like the kind you feel when your car goes down a hill too fast. She looked out the window and realized the plane was starting to descend. She could see the sun had just set, and the sky was a beautiful shade of orange and purple with light, hazy wisps of gray.

It was an odd feeling to read her mother's past. She had only read a few pages and learned three things she did not know: her mother had been in a childhood drunk driving accident that had claimed the life of her best friend; her grandfather was an asshole; and the bus her mother took from Ohio and Utah was nowhere near as fancy and plush as the Greyhound she had always thought it to be.

She had never known any details of her mother's childhood or that Kay's father had abused her. As saddened as this news was, it intrigued her, and she wanted to read more. Lauren's mother was rather tight-lipped when it came to her past, so never in million years would she have thought the woman would write a tell-all, but it was right there in her hand. It was all so shocking, and Lauren began to wonder if her mother had left it behind on purpose—a way to tell her story without having to stand there face to face.

When Lauren's flight landed in Heathrow, she checked her voicemail. Lo and behold, there was Kay's frantic voice. "Uh, Lauren, honey, this is Mom. I was just wondering if you found, uh...file folder—you know, in our hotel room. It must have fallen on the floor or something. I know you probably won't get this—I mean, uh, until you land—but let me know if you have the file with you. It's kind of important, honey, and I... Well, just let me know as soon as you can." Clearly, Lauren's mother had no intention of anyone reading her personal file, whether it was a hotel maid or her own daughter.

27

Lauren hoped not many people would be boarding the flight at Heathrow so she could continue her journey without having to share her space. After several passengers left the plane, she got up to use the restroom. When she returned, she saw that only a few passengers were boarding, much to her relief, but one of them had occupied the seat next to her. She looked around and realized there was a row of empty seats in the very back of the plane, so she politely excused herself, grabbed her belongings—and her mother's—and took over the back row. She settled into her new space and turned on the reading light above her. She was obsessed now and could not stop reading. She'll never know, Lauren told herself. I'll just act like I never looked at it, and it will be my little secret—something she'd always been good at keeping, especially from her mother.

4

After five grueling days of driving, the old bus was finally making the steep climb into the Rockies. Kay was excited about seeing real mountains. After living so close to the Appalachians herself, but never actually getting to see them, this almost seemed to make the trip worth all torment. Her father had driven the whole way. Bart wasn't any help, he was a waste. He sat on the stairs of the bus entry and drank beer the entire trip. He might as well have stayed in Ohio.

When they reached the fifth day of their trek, Kay's father and mother began talking about Mormonism. They warned their children to stay as far away from the cult as possible and told them they were—in no way, shape, or form—to date, marry, fraternize with, or go to any events hosted by the Mormons. It was made crystal clear, especially by John, that they would be punished if they got involved with the cult.

Kay wasn't sure what her parents were talking about. She pictured people with painted faces dancing around a fire, spouting some "Hooga Booga" kind of chant. But her fathers' threats caused enough fear that she made the promise to stay away from the 'cult'.

As they drove along I-80, her father talked to truckers over the CB radio. Throughout the trip, a variety of gruff-voiced truckers mentioned how cool the crappy old bus was. Over time, John became concerned with the brakes on the bus and the fact that there was no power steering already didn't help. It was early October, so there wasn't any bad weather to speak of, but the bus was old and stubborn and difficult to steer, and he kept mentioning the canyons that he would have to maneuver and hoped the brakes would last through them.

Her father seemed to become very nervous as they approached the Wasatch Mountains. Using the CB radio

29

he asked some truckers if they would help him navigate the old bus through the canyon. As the bus swerved and swayed its way through the pass, Kay was only able to see shadows of the looming mountains; she could not wait till daylight to get the full picture.

They were headed to Fruit Heights, an elite little town located on the bench of the Wasatch Mountains, just thirty miles north of Salt Lake City. The neighborhoods in that area were surrounded by cherry orchards, and that was where Uncle Hal and his wife lived. Kay knew them pretty well because Hal and his family visited Ohio each year and stayed with Kay's grandmother. They were the only part of Kay's family who did not live in Ohio, and they just happened to be Mormon.

John's Uncle Hal had suggested that the family should move to Utah because there were more job opportunities there. What Hal was really trying to say was that it was time for John to grow up and get away from his drinking buddies so he could focus on treating his family better. Intrigued by the chance at a different life, John took Hal up on his offer and flew to Utah. He stayed with Hal and Carol for a month until he landed his new job.

Hal and Carol had been waiting for days for John and the family to arrive, and they had no idea it would be in a big old bus. They lived in a beautiful neighborhood, and they were clearly taken aback by the early-morning arrival of the hillbilly bus. John and his entourage looked like a band of hippies. For Kay, the worst part of the trip was arriving in a place she had never been and having to see the mortified faces of Hal and Carol as they gawked at that ugly brown bus and the family disembarking from it. None of them had showered since they left Ohio, which was bad enough, but it was even more embarrassing that John had brought his nasty alcoholic friend and his big smelly hunting dog along.

Hal and Carol did their best to make Kay and her brother Luke feel at home. However, Kay could tell it was an awkward situation for everyone. Sometimes it hit her that she would not being going home anytime soon and when it did, she cried because she missed her old life. If her father heard her crying, he would yell at her to stop. There was no compassion for Kay, and her feelings were not allowed to be felt or acknowledged. For this reason, Kay had a difficult time speaking up; constantly afraid she might get in trouble. She knew that even the sound of her voice sent her father reeling in anger. It had always been uncomfortable for her when he was around, but the older she got, the more aware she became of it.

Within several weeks of arriving in Fruit Heights and living with Hal and Carol, Suzanne went to work as a secretary in an accounting office. That enabled them to have enough money to eventually find a place to rent.

John finally felt he had found the perfect place for his family to settle, in a small town called Heber. He could not wait to show Suzanne, and she was excited to get them settled into a home of their home again. By that time, Hal and Carol were just as eager for them to go as they were to have a place of their own.

* * *

Several days before John took the family to see the house he had found for them, there had been a late autumn blizzard, pummeling the Wasatch front with snow. It hit especially hard in the mountains and Heber, the small town they were ready to move to. It was a bitter cold, long drive twenty miles up through the canyon, but Kay and Luke couldn't have been more excited. They were going to live in the mountains.

John had kept the bus with all of their belongings parked at a cousin's house in Ogden. In the meantime, he had scraped together enough money to buy an old white 1963 Ford Falcon for one hundred dollars. It had red scratchy material on the seats and smelled like gas, but it got them around from place to place. Kay and Luke sat in the back seat of the smelly old car as it slipped and slid its

31

way up a long a gravel driveway that was snow packed and covered in a thick sheet of ice.

As they inched their way closer to their destination, Kay could make out a blue house in the distance. There was so much snow that it was difficult to tell right away, but the house looked as though it had a black roof. As they got closer, she realized it was not black, but burnt. Clearly, the house had been in a fire.

In spite of its crispy roof that reminded Kay of burnt toast, John was excited about the place. He yelled out, "Don't you love it? Come on! I'll show ya the inside." The family was speechless as they watched John in all his glory, pointing out that there had been a fire and it had burned the bathroom and kitchen area, but he was going to rebuild the home. To him, it was heaven.

Kay could not believe her eyes and ears. They were standing in three feet of snow, in what was supposed to be their living room, and her father was happy. They had all been through months of losing so much and living off others in order to avoid homelessness, and now it looked as if they really were going to be homeless. Then things got worse.

Suzanne immediately broke down crying and asked John, "Just exactly how are we supposed to live here?"

John was immediately pissed off, as usual, and yelled, "Oh shut the hell up and stop worrying." He told her he had another surprise for her and that it would make her happy. He walked her out the back door of the half-burned home, at the bottom of a slope there it was: an old white mobile home with streaks of rust and covered in snow. It rested just along the edge of a river. John and Luke seemed to be the only ones excited about it.

Luke thought it the whole place was exceptionally cool. He didn't seem to mind that there was an actual fire and that there was a huge hole burned through the ceiling. He just ran around through knee-high snow in his new home, happy as could be.

Kay and her mother, on the hand, were clearly disappointed. When they were met with a mobile home that was older than the bus he had relocated them in, Suzanne began to cry even harder. Kay became frightened, knowing that Suzanne might trigger the crazed lunatic in her father to come out. She kept trying to console her mother, telling her everything would be okay, even though she knew it was going to be horrible. She would have to become even more creative in her daydreaming. Her dream world was a place that she built because of her father, but now the misery of reality had gone to a whole new level.

Luke and Kay were never really close because John callously managed to drive a wedge between them. Over time, Luke was programmed to believe Kay was bad. Somehow, though, they adjusted. The old mobile home became a livable environment, and the two kids learned to adapt to their new school and their lives in Heber.

* * *

Luckily, they had to start school right away because they were months behind from the move. Kay was in fifth grade and Luke in third. The first day of school was difficult for Kay. In Ohio, she would have been in middle school, but in Utah, she still had two more years of elementary before going into junior high.

There wasn't really any further discussion about the cult that was so abruptly and briefly discussed on the bus. Living in Utah as a poor non-Mormon, Kay realized immediately she did not have a lot of choices when it came to friends. It was a lonely new world. Her parents had only warned her about staying away from the Mormons and hadn't explained that the entire state was consumed by them. Suddenly Kay was confused by adults, classmates, and teachers asking if Kay and her family had found something called a Ward She had no idea that a Ward was a specific Mormon church in the area where your home is

33

located. She was clueless, and it did not even occur to her that these questions had anything to do with the cult her father had warned her to stay away from. She wanted and needed friends. She was eleven years old, sad and lonely, and she missed her old life terribly. She needed compassion—something she was not getting at home. She did not want people to come over to the property or see the trailer she lived in next to a burned-out house that her father never seemed to find the time to rebuild. Months passed as Kay avoided people and the questions they had about her life and religion. She could not understand. It was as if they spoke a whole other language.

Finally, after Kay had spent months trying to fit in, a girl named Chanin invited her to come over and hang out at her home. Kay walked right by Chanin's home every day, and they were in the same class together. Kay accepted Chanin's invitation and started going to Chanin's after school every day, and the girls became close friends.

Weeks turned to months, and Chanin's home became more like Kay's home away from home. She never wanted to go to her old trailer where Bart, her father's friend, was still hanging around. For the most part, Kay was left alone by her family, so she spent a lot of time at Chanin's. Her home was beautiful and clean, with new carpet. It had a microwave, something Kay had not seen or used before. Almost every day after school, the girls would microwave hot dogs, play games, and do their homework. Kay found a place where she could get swallowed up into another person's life, and that helped her forget how much she missed everyone in Ohio. During those hours, it was as if the move never happened, and she finally experienced a little peace of mind.

One night, Kay was asked to sleep over at Chanin's. She was excited and expected they would play cards or watch a movie. Instead, Chanin was had a special treat for Kay, a presentation that her and her mother worked hard to put together. It was quite a production. She had poster board, music, and books ready to explain the story of a boy called Joseph Smith. It wasn't long before Kay realized what Chanin was trying to teach her. "Oh, yes, I know about this!" she said excitedly. "This is about the cult my father told me about."

Chanin immediately broke into tears and ran out of her bedroom to get her mom, who then explained to Kay it was inappropriate to call a religion a cult. "Cult is a bad word," she said before she asked if she could meet with Kay's mother.

This scared Kay; she didn't think she had done anything wrong. After all, her father was the one who had used the word "cult". She did not want to lose a friend, and she was terrified to think what would happen if John found out she was hanging out with the Mormons.

It was awkward and uncomfortable, but a day was chosen for Kay's and Chanin's mothers to meet. The visit went surprisingly well, and Kay's mom asked if Chanin could sleep over with Kay. Chanin's mom agreed based on the agreement that neither of them were to discuss religion. So that weekend, Chanin came over with her sleeping bag. She had no idea she would be camping out in a trailer.

Within the hour John returned home with Bart in tow. They were drunk, as usual, and started cursing and hollering.

Immediately, Chanin asked if she could go home, and Kay pleaded, "No, please don't go."

Chanin insisted and told Kay she was not feeling well and wanted to call her mother to come get her. Kay could see that Chanin was visibly shaken by the alcoholics who were smoking in the trailer. It was completely normal to Kay, but no matter how much Kay tried to reassure Chanin, she still wanted to leave.

Kay was angry when Chanin left. It was her first chance to have a real friend, and she realized John was ruining everything for her. She did not know if Chanin would ever want to speak to her or hang out with her again. She buried her face into her pillow, and cried herself to sleep.

Several days passed, and Kay's mother called Chanin's mother to apologize for John's careless behavior, but it was too late. Chanin was banned from coming over to Kay's home.

John and Bart had left for several days to go on a so called hunting trip. When they returned, Bart was very drunk. John had to get some clean clothes and get back to work. He left Bart at the trailer with Kay and her brother Luke. The siblings began arguing about something ridiculous, and Bart decided to intervene. He picked up Kay and threw her out of the trailer, where she hit her head on a rock and began bleeding. Luke was in shock and frightened. He immediately called his mother, and she rushed home. She kicked Bart out and told him if he ever came back, she would call the police. Since Suzanne was working every day to bring in extra money, she had no idea the amount of abuse Kay and Luke were subjected to at the cruel hands of their father and Bart.

* * *

Things got progressively worse after Bart left. John, upset with the family's financial struggles, began drinking even more heavily, and things quickly grew worse in Utah than they had been in Ohio. Even John knew the family was quickly heading toward its doom. After ten months of living in Utah, with the family not fitting into the environment that surrounded them and no real hope of making a decent living, John felt it was time to pack up the bus and go back to Ohio. Suzanne agreed, and while the kids were sleeping, they went outside to get the bus ready to go. When they walked over to where the bus had been parked on the other side of the property, they discovered that someone had bashed in the windshield and that most of the passenger windows had had rocks thrown through them. At that moment, they realized they were stuck—that life was trying to tell them to stay put. As bad as things were, they took it as a sign that if they stayed where they were, everything would somehow work out. Right then and there, John promised to be a better father and husband.

* * *

Surprisingly, changes did start to happen. The man even started to attend church with Suzanne, and she began making Kay and her brother attend as well. Suzanne and John hadn't attended church in years, and Kay was just confused about religion period. There was no structure, and she did not understand why the Mormons were considered so bad since their families seemed so cohesive and family oriented. They had family get-togethers, and though it was strange to Kay, their homes were much more peaceful than her own. She was growing up and seeing things in a different light. Her mother had chosen to attend a Baptist church, and they were all baptized within several months.

After that, things started to get better. John had calmed down, and there was not as much fear in the home. This took some pressure off Kay. It was easier for her to pretend they were Mormon as long as she had a mother and a father that did not smoke or drink. John had even gotten a better job working on Hill Air Force Base, forty-five miles from their home. They were making more money, and John started to rebuild the old house. He had made a deal with the landlord to fix the house up in exchange for free rent and then eventually they would buy the home. Kay and her brother each had their own rooms downstairs, and her mother and father slept upstairs.

With the money they were making and the holiday season rolling around, John decided after a long year and half to go back to Ohio for a visit. That was the best news Kay had heard in all her twelve years. She was about to go on her first airplane ride and see her grandmother's and cousins again. She could not believe it. She barely slept the night before they left. Her father was so excited he hugged the whole family that night before they went to bed. It was truly the first and only time Kay could ever remember him being happy.

Finally, after years of watching airplanes crisscrossing the sky, Kay was going to know what it felt like to fly. She was so elated and full of butterflies. She was even more thrilled to hear they would have to take two different flights to get there. It was the most exciting moment of Kay's life, and she could not wait to see her cousins and her grandmothers again.

It was a wonderful trip, the best time of her life. For the first time in two years, Kay felt accepted again and safe. She could be herself in Ohio, and she loved every minute of it.

For the whole visit, Suzanne and the kids spent their time visiting with family, but John drank away the hours at the Legion. He had not had a drink for months and wanted to take advantage of every moment he had with his old buddies. As a result, by the time they all left for the airport, they were back to square one with John: cussing, abusive, angry, and always nursing a liquor bottle.

Kay did not want to go back to Utah after it was over. She cried off and on the entire trip, begging her parents to let her stay, telling them she missed Ohio and her family there—especially her grandmother. Ohio was her home, and having to return to Utah made no sense to her. The Mormons may have liked it, but it was hell to her.

When they got back to Utah, John was not around much. On the rare occasion that he was, Kay and even Luke were afraid of him, especially when their mother was at work. He was short tempered and mean as hell. At one point, he even lifted Luke up by his feet and held him over the cliff behind their home and yelled, "Boy, you know I could drop you right now on your head, and you would die!"

Kay had never seen Luke so petrified. The abuse was usually directed at her, and to see it happening to Luke was pure madness.

Luke and Kay began to grow closer as their father's wrath raged on. They tried to spend as much time as possible outside riding their bikes up and down the street near their property. One afternoon a large diesel moving truck was coming down the road as Kay was riding ahead of Luke. She decided to ride to the corner and wait there for the diesel to pass or turn so she could cross the street. As the diesel started to turn, each trailer hitched to the truck came closer and closer to the curb. Luke watched in horror as eventually Kay was swallowed up by the third trailer. Her bike slid under the truck wheels and was bent into a pretzel. Luke could see the bike and thought for a moment that Kay had been run over, but Kay had pushed herself away from trailer and off her bike, she was lying in the briar bushes near the curb crying. Her arm was scraped by the truck, and her legs were bleeding from the briars. Luke immediately ran home to get help.

John came walking down the street to where Kay was lying, and he was laughing out loud.

Luke was shocked. *He's our dad. How could he laugh at a time like this? What's so funny?*

John picked up the bike and said, "Well, I guess you don't have a bike anymore. That was real smart."

Kay and Luke were both devastated, but they wouldn't find any comfort at home. It was as if it never happened, even though Kay was traumatized by her near-death experience. To make matters worse and add to Kay's anxiety, her Mormon neighbors had witnessed her father's disregard for her and saw how unconcerned he was for her after the accident.

For months, Kay had nightmares that she had slipped and fallen in the other direction under the truck and her head was smashed by the truck tires. She would wake up crying, and her mother and father would both just tell her, "Shut up and go back to bed." Kay began daydreaming again, more often and deeper than ever.

Whenever she heard her father come home from work, she hid under her bed or sometimes she would climb out the window after he checked her room and thought she was gone. She would sneak out to avoid the risk of being beaten just for being in his sight, or worse.

It was becoming more and more uncomfortable being around John. She could even see it in Luke eyes, and they both had a verifiable reason to be worried. All Kay wanted was a normal family, one that was not going to scare off every friend that happened to be Mormon.

She had made a new friend named Noel, and Noel's family lived very much by the Book of Mormon. Noel loved to come over to Kay's home to watch her television, something her family prohibited.

One day when Noel was sitting in Kay's living room, John came home and yelled at Kay, "Did you fucking clean up your room?"

Noel jumped up, looked frightened, and said, "I have to go!"

Once again, John had scared off another friend. He knew Noel was Mormon, and he found scaring little Mormon kids to be thoroughly entertaining.

After twelve years of abuse, a frightened, lonely Kay yelled at her father. "I hate you! I hate you!" she screamed in a rage, holding back tears.

John knew it was because of Noel going home, so he just laughed it off, but Kay was serious. She had had enough of keeping quiet and allowing him to bully her and her innocent friends. The pain he had caused her for most of her childhood was pouring out of her twelve-year-old body, and she wasn't about to let up. She just kept crying and yelling at him.

He finally jumped off the couch and grabbed Kay as she started to run. John had her by the neck and began started choking her. He then threw her like a ragdoll across the master bedroom, causing her to hit her head on the headboard and fall onto the bed.

Just as John was ready to grab her again, out of nowhere her mother Suzanne jumped on John's back and started yelling, "You leave my kids alone!" and began hitting her husband as hard as she could.

Kay in was in a daze and could not believe what she was seeing. Thirteen years of marriage, and her mother never said one word in defense. John seemed stunned for a moment, and Kay was hurting and petrified. *What is he going to do next?*

Suzanne continued to yell, "Get the hell of here, you mother-fucking asshole! It is over! I am not going to let you kill my children!"

He turned and walked out of the bedroom, realizing that was the final straw.

It never occurred to Kay why it had taken so long for Suzanne to stand up for herself and her kids. Suzanne did not want to rock the boat on the illusion of a happy family. Now she realized that family was an impossibility, and she had hit her breaking point.

Lauren had just spent the last hour glued to the pages that were revealing her mother's past, as if it were yesterday. She had been fighting back tears, feeling bad for her mother. She was clueless her mother had been so affected by being a non-Mormon and that her grandfather Whitley had been so brutal and insensitive, to say the least.

She was interrupted as the flight attendant offered her a drink and some dinner. Even though the dry turkey sandwich and chips were not all that enticing, Lauren decided it best to take a small break from her heart-wrenching look at her mother's pained yesteryears. As she and looked out the window, she noticed the sunlight was gone. The only light she could see now was the one flashing on the wing of the plane. She still had many hours to pass before her arrival in New York. She was so bewildered by what she was reading, like a story about someone she had never met.

Growing up, Lauren was always bothered by how much her mother seemed to go overboard in complimenting her about how beautiful she was and how much she loved her. It always seemed slightly exaggerated and insincere somehow, but now she understood. Her mother was compensating for something she herself had longed to hear, and she wanted to make absolutely sure Lauren had no doubts about her love. She felt horrible for silently accusing her mother's attempts of being false. That love was a gift—a gift of compassion and undying care that Kay never got from her own parents. As Lauren chewed the last dry bite of turkey with mayo, she was mesmerized by this woman—her mother—that she seemed to know very little about, and she wanted to read more.

5

The last thing Kay wanted any of her friends to know was that her parents were getting a divorce. It was bad enough putting up a front that she had a normal, peaceful home in order to keep it from being obvious that they were non-Mormons; it would be harder to hide that fact now that her father wasn't coming home. She figured she would just have to learn to pretend even more and hold it all inside as she had always done. Every day, she played the perfect little girl in fear that she may lose all connections to the few friends she had left. She did not want to become what the Mormons called "ex-communicated." She had overheard the parents of her Mormon friends discussing families that had been ex-communicated for not following the doctrine. All she wanted was to fit in, no matter the lies that had to be told.

After her father moved out, Kay's mother began smoking, and they stopped attending the Baptist church where they had become members. That threw Kay into a rage. Not only did she have to hide the fact that her parents had separated, but now she had to hide her mother's nicotine habit as well. Even that wasn't the worst of it though. Another man began showing up at the house quite regularly, her mother's boss. His name was Mark, and he was a nice man, but he made Kay uncomfortable. The best story she could come up with to fool her friends was that her father was out of town on business and Mark was from the church they attended. She told them he would come by to check in and visit with her mother the same way a deacon of their Ward would.

By this time, Kay was thirteen, and most of the kids she played and hung out in the neighborhood with were younger than her and believed everything she told them. She spent hours playing at their homes with them, and they all came from serious, staunch Mormon families. Most of the families had from five to ten children, and the mothers always seemed to be pregnant. Many of them used picnic tables instead of regular kitchen tables or dinettes because there was not enough room or money for chairs. To Kay, the large families were fun. There was never a dull moment, and there was always love, even in the midst of all the mayhem. Kay found it fascinating to see the interaction and drama between all the children; it took her mind off of what was happening in her home. She was always invited to eat at their homes, even though they had little money and sometimes had to eat just buttered toast and milk for dinner. Cult or not, Kay loved the world they lived in and even envied it.

Several of the older girls always wanted to go to Kay's home so they could watch television since none of them had one in their home. But she never felt comfortable having them over and always tried to rush them out when she knew her mother would be returning home.

Mark started to spend the night often, and it was becoming increasingly difficult for Kay to lie to her friends and tell them he was just a priest and that her father would be home soon. The neighbors and children's parents were catching on that Kay's mother was having an affair and that John was not coming home. They banned their children from playing with Kay, and as a result, she became very depressed.

In spite of Kay's uncomfortable feeling about him coming into their lives, Mark was a nice man, from Texas. He was not Mormon and was only living in Utah because he had been promoted to the position of director in the large accounting firm where Kay's mother worked. He was a very down-to-Earth man. He smoked and drank occasionally but was not an extremist like her father. It was strange for Kay to witness a nice, kind man who had no affiliation with Mormonism. Kay had always been on pins and needles around men, and she was caught off guard by Mark's caring, sensitive demeanor.

On the rare occasions when she and Luke saw their father, John would make derogatory comments about Mark. "He is just manipulating you, and he is stupid. He is a weird man. He is using your mom. I don't trust him, and you shouldn't either," he would say. He would blame Mark for his and Suzanne's separation.

This only made it more difficult for Kay to accept Mark as a nice guy, let alone a possible father figure. She was like a puppy that had been beaten her whole life, and she did not trust anyone that wanted to love or care for her or her needs. After all the years of abuse, Kay still did not realize her father was wrong or that he had done anything immoral or illegal. She truly believed his lies, and she always felt she was inadequate because he made her feel that way. So, she believed there must have been a catch, some ulterior motive to Mark's acts of kindness. All sorts of dark thoughts ran through Kay's mind. *Is this so-called nice man just using, my mother?* He had money, and he seemed to love her mother. This seemed strange to Kay, as she had never witnessed affection between her mother and father. It confused her and left her suspicious and uneasy. Kay couldn't trust love—especially from any man.

Kay had hidden many memories and was in denial about many unspoken moments with John. It was not something she couldn't discuss with anyone, ever. She felt nobody would listen anyway because she was always ignored. Besides that, John told her if she said a word to anybody, he would kill her. So, she grew up feeling that any man touching or hugging their child "lovingly" was awkward and wrong. When Mark tried to hug Kay, she felt uncomfortable and did not know how to react; to her, it felt like an improper sexual advance. Embracing was something new after thirteen years of being shoved away from any innocent parental affection. She was hard wired from all the abuse she'd suffered.

Mark asked her questions, talked nicely to her, and wanted to take her shopping. It was all strange territory to her, as John had always been completely opposite and

45

against buying anything new for her. Once, and only once, had she risked asking John for something, a pair of jeans. She explained that everyone at school was wearing them, and she needed them in order to help her fit in. John would not, under any circumstances, give her money to buy them. She was scolded for even asking, as if she had committed a crime. But she had to ask him, she he had to try. Everyone was making fun of her because she did not have any nice clothes. She wore gauchos almost every day. Kay had a hard time getting along with Mark. She could not comprehend why a man she did not know would want to buy her things when her own father wouldn't.

Mark could not understand why Kay had such a hard time with accepting normal love and affection and pulled away if he tried to give her a hug. He finally just let her do her own thing, realizing that pushing the ragged, emotional child was not going to work. He tried his best. He knew Kay wanted some Levi 501s and bought her three pairs to try and win some of her trust. He had no idea of her past and the damage that had been done at the hand of her father.

* * *

Suzanne and Mark were having the time of their lives. Suzanne was so in love, and the last thing on her mind was Kay and her past life or issues. Suzanne was relieved she had finally found love after years of suffering her own abuse from a husband who was never there and never faithful. She had no intention of bringing up or discussing the past. It was not long before the divorce was final. It was very obvious that Mark wanted to marry Suzanne.

Kay found out that her father had been living off and on with someone named Gina for at least a year. He had met her shortly after they moved to Utah and was with

46

her off and on up until the moment Suzanne told him to leave after seeing him hurt Kay.

Mark had two children, a boy and a girl. Sheri and Vance were excited to meet Kay and Luke. They loved their father Mark and wanted to come and live with him in Utah. Sheri was older than Kay and Luke and lived in Texas with her mother, but for some reason, she wanted to be near her father. This puzzled Kay.

Kay met her stepsister for the first time at the wedding, which happened the day after the divorce from John was finalized. It was all so crazy to Kay, and things seemed to be moving at warp speed. One minute they were moving to Utah, and in the next, her mother was marrying another man. Things were discombobulated, and it was difficult to keep up with the pace. Kay was confused and angry, as well as going through puberty. She could barely comprehend one thing before the next blow would hit, sending her back to square one—alone again and dreaming of a good life, the kind with the white house with black shutters, two little boys in their blue room and two little girls in their pink one. But every time she went back to that imaginary dream world in her head, it seemed to be fading. It wasn't sticking with her like before. Reality was setting in, gobbling up her fantasies, and there was no shutting down the truth any longer. She was getting older and wiser.

* * *

Suzanne and Mark decided to find a home of their own, away from Heber, and they started house hunting. In the meantime, Kay was finally starting to feel safe without John around. She was able to test the waters, speaking up, acting out, or even sometimes goofing off. She was finally able to let her emotions flow, and the fear was subsiding, but Kay always felt insecure. She was very sensitive and emotional. She could not control her emotions, and Mark,

47

who didn't understand her past, just assumed she was crazy—a problem child.

Kay had become very edgy and high strung. She was very thin and pale, and she looked malnourished. She could eat a dozen donuts daily and not gain one pound. She was as thin as a rail for age thirteen, and as white as a ghost. Her brown hair had become full of natural curls as she had gotten older, and just before John moved out, she'd gotten braces. She was going through an awkward stage, and up until she met Mark's daughter Sheri, she was never one to look in the mirror much, and she was relatively unaware of her own presence. Sheri was sixteen, going on seventeen and was most definitely a girly girl. She took Kay under her wing and showed her how to do her hair, pluck her eyebrows and use makeup. Kay loved having an older sister who could take time to help her adapt through puberty.

Unfortunately, it wasn't long before Sheri became homesick for Texas and wanted to finish her senior year in Dallas. After she left, Kay took the little knowledge she had acquired from Sheri and used it to the best of her ability.

The family found a home they bought together in Kaysville, Utah. It was a large, beautiful home in a very distinguished neighborhood. Kay felt as if she had landed on another planet or moved to another state once again. It was a six-bedroom, three-bathroom home with two kitchens: one upstairs and a small one downstairs. It was so new and big that Luke and Kay were both in a state of shock. It took them time to adjust once again to new surroundings. All that mattered to Kay was that she had a fresh start in a place where nobody knew about her past.

* * *

Kay began going to Kaysville Junior High in the middle of her seventh-grade year. She had high expectations for a new start in a new place, but on her first day, she immediately started to get teased and called "Shitley." It was horrible! She wanted to change her last name to Mark's name, Kelley, but her mother would not let her for fear of how John might react. So, Kay (and Luke, for that matter) had to endure the name Whitley and its nasty rhyming counterpart all over again. It was like the past would not stop following her.

It did not take Kay long to find a boy worth noticing, and when she did, she quickly developed a mad crush on him. His name was Justin, and she could not stop thinking about him. She knew he was Mormon, but at this point, after several years of living in Utah, she realized it was becoming less and less of an issue and there was little to be afraid of. It was just reality. She rode her bike past Justin's house all the time. To her, no other boy existed, and she would fantasize and talk about him for the next two years, even though he just teased her like all the other kids and called her just as many nasty names.

All of Kay's girlfriends knew she liked Justin and hoped eventually he would come to like her. They all thought he teased her because he had a secret crush on her. Kay was extremely sensitive. She had been through so much and wanted to fit in and be accepted. Her non-Mormon upbringing was just one extra hurdle to overcome. Comments about her name or what she wore made break down and cry. Justin and his friends knew that and took advantage, going so far as to see who could make her cry first. Despite this cruelty, Kay could not help how she felt. She liked Justin so much and hoped he would come around and start liking her too. She wanted to be around him as much as possible, even though he was a jerk to her. She desperately hoped he would eventually see the light—notice her undying loyalty and infatuation—and ask to be her boyfriend. But all of her romantic dreams with

Justin came to a crushing defeat on a Saturday afternoon toward the end of ninth grade.

Justin and three of his friends were riding their bikes through Kay's neighborhood. Kay and her friend Robin saw them and decided to follow them. The boys stopped at a convenience store to buy some drinks, Robin and Kay went inside to buy some candy, and they all ended up outside talking in the parking lot. The teasing began, but Kay fought back. She started to yell at Cory, one of Justin's good friends. Cory walked over and grabbed her from her bike, picked her up, and threw her into a dumpster that sat next to the store. She landed at the bottom of the smelly dumpster, on top of damp, broken-down large boxes and miscellaneous other trash. She tried to get out and couldn't, even with Robin trying to help. The boys ganged up on the girls; they pushed Robin down and slammed the lids of the dumpster closed. Kay was trapped!

She could hear lots of laughter from the boys, and she could make out Robin yelling, "Let her out of there! Get her out!" Instead, the boys did the unthinkable. Kay was crying, trying to lift one of the lids to get out, but the boys jumped up on top of it. Suddenly, she could see water dripping between the lids. She was screaming, demanding that they let her out when finally they jumped off. Kay was able to push open the left side of the lid, and with the help of a store employee, she managed to climb out. The whole time the boys were on the ground, holding their sides and rolling with laughter.

She then heard the words that would change her life forever: "Justin pissed on you!"

Kay was shocked speechless when she realized the liquid that had come through the space of the lids and splattered on her when it hit the cardboard boxes was the piss of the boy she liked—as if it wasn't humiliating enough that they had tossed her in the dumpster to begin with. They boys rode off on their bikes while Kay and Robin walked theirs home. Kay was in shock and crying.

Robin felt horrible for her heartbroken and humiliated friend, and was devastated herself by the cruelty and disregard she had witnessed. It was the worst thing anyone had ever done to Kay, outside of her own family abuse.

For her, it was as if the world stopped spinning. *How could he have done that to me?* She wondered. She had chased after him for two years. She had dreamt of marrying him someday and had desperately hoped he had or would develop feelings for her, but her dreams about Justin had turned into a nightmare.

She went home and spent the next day in bed. It was Sunday, and she did not want to go to school the next day. Her friends told her she had to and the only way to get past the whole thing was to show up, so she did. Kay walked through the front door of the school, but before she could even reach her locker, she could hear somebody say, "Kay got pissed on!" Feeling weak and depressed and unable to move, she turned and walked out of the school, feeling like she was ruined and her life was over. She made it home, crawled into her bed, and cried for days.

Her mother was very concerned. She had heard what had happened through Luke, who had heard about the incident from his friends. Suzanne wanted so badly to call Justin's mother and father, but Kay begged her not to, explaining that it would only make things worse.

Kay did not return to school for weeks. She spent hours in the bathtub and in bed. It was a month before school was out, and then she would be off to high school. There, four middle schools that would be merging, but she wondered how much of her past would run over into her future. It was something she spent the summer dwelling on.

As she read on, imagining the horror of a teenage girl trapped and humiliated in a dumpster by the boy she loved, Lauren was mortified and embarrassed for her mother. She could not believe she was even able to write down and reveal something so horrific.

Lauren put the notebook down for a moment, needing a few minutes to process all the grim details of her mother's most difficult adolescence. It seemed like a fictional story—like some heartbreaking Sunday afternoon movie you might catch on Lifetime. She had known her mother had moved from Ohio to Utah at a young age, but she did not know she had been teased and had endured such abuse and cruel bullying. Lauren herself had never been through anything remotely like it. She was always accepted and well liked.

Lauren had a calm, cool, and collected demeanor that naturally drew people to her. It was hard for her to even comprehend being bullied or to fathom what would drive anyone to treat another person—especially her mother—so badly. Hey, I'm the only one who's allowed to pick on my mom! She thought. Why was my mother so abused? As far back as she could remember, her mother had always been extremely sensitive, but with a strong exterior, in order to hide her pain. Now, with these painful revelations, Kay's attitude and emotions were starting to make more sense to Lauren.

As a flight attendant walked past, Lauren asked her for a pillow and blanket. She situated herself as comfortably as one can on a cramped airplane and continued reading, wanting to know more about this woman she'd come from.

6

Kay hated school. For her, it was the most painful thing to sit in a room all day long and listen to someone prattle on and on. She had become anxious and impatient and could not sit still. She had been a good elementary student in Ohio, but things were different in Utah. She was constantly made fun, whether it was her name, her clothes or her good grades. She would sometimes be perceived as the teacher's pet. She had given up trying to do well in school. She thought it best to stay under the radar, so her classmates might ignore her. Academically, Kay did not and could not focus and as a result, her grades fell way below average.

Kay entered high school it was her sophomore year. She soon realized that there were many more people than she thought there would be. Her new classmates had no idea who she was and what she had been through at Kaysville Junior High. It was only when she saw particular Kaysville Junior High students that her stomach would turn.

She had acquaintances and a couple of close friends. Most of them were considered "Jack Mormon," non-practicing Mormons. All of her friends at the time were just trying to adjust to the big differences between high school and junior high or middle school. Kay was praying she would not see anyone or have a class with anyone from Kaysville that knew about her bullied, shameful past. She hoped if she did see anyone, they would not refer to her as "Shitley." But second and more importantly, she hoped they wouldn't say, "Look! It's the girl who got pissed on!"

It was a crap shoot the first week of high school. She wondered if it would really be as bad as she thought it would be. Mainly, she hoped she did not have any classes

53

with Justin or his friends. She never wanted to see him again after what he had done to her. She was finally over her obsession with him, for that obsession had been replaced. Now she was obsessed with keeping her past a secret.

It was pure luck she did not have one class with him or his evil minions. Each time she entered a new classroom, she would look for him or any of his partners in crime. She had a plan that if she had a class or classes with any of them, she would request a schedule change. It was horrible the pain and embarrassment that Kay had to live with, something no one should ever have to endure. She was a strong girl and was able to hold up under a lot of pressure due to her abusive childhood with John the maniac. After all, it had only been about two years earlier she was beaten and tossed around by him. She had a strong imagination that seemed to pull her through the hell she had been living in since birth. Her daydreaming was becoming more and more prevalent.

Kay dreaded going to school, and after the events that took place that year, she could barely stand to be in the same building with the people who had been so cruel to her. She constantly worried that when she would turn a corner in the hall, one of the boys would be there to make it clear to all the students who she was—that she had been pissed on by Justin Roberts. It was a nightmare. As much as she hoped her past would not come back to haunt her, within just a few weeks of starting at the new school, several people here and there would point and whisper as she walked by them or they would say some cruel things about Kay, she did her best to pretend they weren't there.

* * *

For Kay, the weekends were not much better. She did her best to make excuses to avoid being sent to see her biological father John. Her brother Luke would always want to go, so at least once a month, Kay had to go spend a weekend in Heber. By that time, John lived with his girlfriend Gina and her seven-year-old daughter Jill. He and Gina fought like cats and dogs. She was a spicy Italian and would not allow him to push her around like Suzanne had allowed. Kay got along with Gina, and it made it somewhat easier to go to visit her father knowing Gina would be there. Gina made her feel at least a little protected.

The only problem was that they all witnessed far too much domestic violence firsthand. Both Luke and Kay felt bad for Jill. John and Gina yelled and cursed at each other nonstop. It was a volatile situation daily, and for little Jill to endure such hell at a young age was entirely wrong.

In late October, John and Gina had driven down to pick up Luke and Kay for the weekend. By the time they reached Kaysville, Luke had become sick with the flu. Kay was left to go visit for the weekend without her brother, something that had never happened before.

That Friday night, Gina, Kay, and Jill went to the grocery store to buy what was needed for the dinner Gina was going to make for them on Saturday night. Gina was a fantastic cook. She worked in the kitchen all day Saturday preparing lasagna and homemade garlic bread and salad. Gina was only twenty-seven years old, just twelve years older than Kay. They bonded, and Gina enjoyed spending time with Kay. They loved to listen to music together; it was quite normal to have Asia or the Eagles playing in the background, the albums Gina usually chose to put on the record player.

Kay had helped set the table. She was so hungry and could not wait to sink her teeth into the meal that Gina had so carefully prepared. She had turned the house into a home with a savory aroma of fresh garlic bread and her Italian sauce. John had gone fishing and out drinking with his buddies most of the afternoon. When he walked in the door, Kay could smell the alcohol, so strong it almost overpowered the scent and aroma of Gina's home cooking at its finest. It was a smell Kay had grown accustomed to when she lived with her father, but for some reason, that evening; it seemed more potent than usual.

Dinnertime finally came around at seven o'clock. Gina snapped at John, "Great! You have been drinking all day again! You are not going to ruin our dinner! Make sure to wash up before you come to the table."

This set him off into a rage. He stomped over to the table where Kay and Jill were already seated and picked up the table and threw it across the kitchen. The meal Kay had been craving to eat was completely wrecked, and the delicious-smelling food was splattered and strewn everywhere. He went to the back door, opened it, and whistled for his hunting dog. Like a wild animal, it ran through the back door and slid into the kitchen. It began to devour the meal Gina had worked so hard to make.

Gina was furious. She started cussing him out and screaming at the top of her lungs, "You fucking asshole! You motherfucker! How dare you!" and began pushing him.

John left the kitchen and walked back in holding his twelve-gauge shotgun. He pointed it at Gina and looked over at Kay and told her to take the truck and go for a drive with Jill.

Gina continued to scream at the top of her lungs, "What are you going to do you stupid asshole? Are you going to shoot me? Fuck you!"

Jill was crying and becoming hysterical as Kay rummaged around looking for the keys. Finally, John reached into his pocket and threw the keys to Kay and yelled at her to go. Kay was fifteen and only had her driver's permit. In spite of the fact that she was petrified, she did as the man holding the gun told her to. She had been on auto-pilot her whole life anyway, especially when it came to John. The man had bullied her, and to her it was just another episode of crazy madness. But this was stepped up to another dimension, one Kay had not witnessed before. It did not even cross her mind to go and get help. She did not think it was an option, and she knew better. If she told anyone, she knew he would beat her or maybe even worse use the shotgun on her. So, she just drove around for what seemed to be an hour. Jill was crying and understandably hysterical the whole time. Kay tried her best to console her, telling her things like "It'll be alright, Jill," or "It will pass. It always does. We just need to drive and let them work it out." They were both so used to John's outbursts and psychotic, drunken ways, but Kay knew this time was pushing the limit.

Kay did not know what to do after they'd driven around for what had to be more than an hour, so she finally drove back to the house, hoping maybe things had calmed down. She told Jill to stay in the truck as she nervously opened the truck door and hopped out. She walked up on the porch and looked in the window to see what was going on inside the house; it was quiet. She opened the front door and stepped inside. It was dark and the only light that was on was in the kitchen. She noticed what she thought to be the pasta sauce splattered on the wall from when her crazy father had flipped the table over, but as she walked into the kitchen and turned the corner, she realized it wasn't marinara sauce she saw. There was Gina, lying on the floor in a pool of blood, right next to a broken plate and a pink-soaked piece of garlic bread the dog had somehow missed in its feeding frenzy.

Kay gasped in horror, petrified and in a state of shock. She did not see her father or know where he was. All she knew was that he was drunk, crazy, and now a possible murderer, and as far as she knew, he still had that shotgun. She just wanted to get out of the house as fast as possible and run for help. She turned around frantically and headed for the front door.

Just as she was ready to open the screen door and run out, she heard her father yell, "Stop!"

She froze. She could sense he was right behind her, sitting on the couch. She could smell the whiskey on his breath from across the room. She knew him too well and knew he would kill her in a heartbeat. No matter how badly she wanted to run, trying to make such a brash move would only make things worse.

"Come in and close the door," her father ordered.

Trembling and feeling as if she were going to pass out, Kay reluctantly started to back up and close the door. Just as she began to slowly turn around, she heard the gun go off. Immediately, she screamed and ducked down, covering her head and curling up into a ball to protect her from the blast that had already taken place. As she was lying on the floor hunched over in sheer pain, she realized the only thing she was suffering from was a bad case of terror. It was not she who had caught the shotgun pellets.

Seconds passed, and she stayed there, frozen in the fetal position and wondering just what her father had shot at if not at her. When the first tiny shard of courage and sanity returned to her, she slowly peeked through her arms that were sheltering her face. For a split second, she thought she was dreaming, but it was all too real. Her father had put the shotgun in his own mouth and pulled the trigger. His head had been blown in half.

She started screaming in horror. Paralyzed by shock, she could not move no matter how badly she wanted to and needed to. She wanted it all to be a bad dream and hoped she would wake up. Somehow, she found her legs and used the wall to help herself up. Her legs collapsed from under her like they were made of rubber bands, so she had to crawl into the kitchen to the phone to dial 911. She was crying to the 911 operator, asking for help. Her heart was beating so hard she could practically see it popping out of her chest.

As her senses returned to her, she realized Gina could still be alive. "Please hurry!" she said to the 911 dispatcher. She then remembered poor little Jill that she left sitting in the truck. "Oh my God!" she screamed. "I have to go check on my sister!"

She dropped the phone and ran outside to tell the little sobbing girl to stay in the truck. She cuddled her in her arms, rocking her, as they waited for help to arrive. She did not want Jill to enter the house and see the bloodbath. Her mother was dying—or maybe dead already—and there was nothing Kay could do. She knew Gina would not want Jill to see her that way. She also knew Gina would want her to watch over the girl and keep her safe, so that is what she did.

When they finally heard the sirens of the approaching police and ambulance, Jill put two and two together and started to scream and cry out, "Mommy! Mommy! What happened to my mommy?"

The pain was so excruciating for Kay. She had seen her father dead and witnessed Jill's mother dying. John had shot Gina in the back, leaving her lying face down in a pool of blood. By the time help arrived, Gina had passed away. Jill was completely in the dark, and Kay could not do or say anything because she was in shock.

The girls were taken to a police station, where Mark and Suzanne picked Kay up. Jill was picked up by her grandmother, and little did Kay know that she would never see her little sister again after that fateful night.

Kay immediately went into denial about the whole situation. The visions of that night had to be buried beneath a new dream, a new life. Kay would not talk about anything or tell anyone, including Mark and Suzanne, what she had witnessed. The police filled them in on what had transpired, but Kay was more concerned about who would find out the truth. She asked them both to tell people in the future that her father and Gina had been killed in a car accident. Only Mark and Suzanne knew the truth: John had shot and killed Gina and then exacted the death penalty on himself. However, they didn't even know the extent of what Kay witnessed or endured that awful evening in Heber.

Lauren had lost it in the middle of the chapter but could not stop reading. She was shaking and could not fight back the tears. She dropped the notebook and immediately went into the lavatory, which was right behind her seat. She closed the door to the small confined space and looked at herself in the mirror. She began sobbing harder as she sank down onto lid of the toilet. An indescribable pain came over her, almost as if her mother had somehow embodied her, and she was feeling the pain that young girl must have felt at the moment she looked upon her father's dead body. She was disillusioned, sad, and angry all at the same time.

Lauren had always been told that Kay had lost her father in a car accident when Kay was a teenager. She had no idea her mother had witnessed or been through such horror. She felt so guilty for being so mean to her mother during her years as a teenager. Lauren had thrown Kay under the bus more times than she could count and was horrified by what she had just read.

After about twenty minutes of crying, she heard the captain over the intercom telling everyone to take their seats and make sure their seatbelts were securely in place, as they were approaching turbulent weather. Disillusioned, she slid open the lavatory door. She noticed the flight attendant standing in the back where the drinks were located. The flight attendant could see that Lauren was visibly upset and asked her if she needed anything before they both had to take their seats. Lauren asked her for a vodka tonic and then crawled back into to her space. She was trapped. It was the middle of the night, somewhere over the Atlantic, and Lauren began to realize that it was going to be impossible for her to keep what she was learning a secret. For the first time in Lauren's life, her mother finally had her full attention.

7

Kay was good at pretending everything was alright, even though she had witnessed horror firsthand. Hiding her emotions was a skill she had mastered. Her brother Luke, however, was devastated at the thought of losing his father. Kay had let her mother and Mark know she did not want anyone to know about her father committing suicide, and she also asked again that her last name could be changed to Kelley, Mark's last name. Things were hard enough, and the last thing she needed was more pressure or to be reminded about something as scandalous as her father's murder-suicide every time she wrote his last name behind hers.

Kay was behaving strangely and began showing up tardy for school or skipping classes altogether. At that time, in the 1980's, post-traumatic stress disorder was unheard of. It was not something Suzanne or Mark were not aware of, and they had no idea how to even begin to help or talk to Kay about the tragedy, so the girl was left to take on the burden alone. She was getting better at daydreaming. She was in another world and began smoking and hanging out with some kids in the back parking lot of the high school. Ironically enough, they smoked right next to the seminary building used for Mormon kids to take the required religious classes throughout their middle school and high school years. Every junior high and high school in Utah had a seminary building.

Kay no longer paid much attention to what was going on around her. She was losing memories of her life in Ohio as a child; they had slipped away, along with the grim recollections of her father's death. She was so used to taking one hit at a time, and even at a young age, she had learned to just subconsciously expect something bad to happen all the time, and it usually did. Unfortunately, her subconscious was catching up to her, even though she tried her best to bury all the memories.

Kay had entered puberty, and after several months of disobedience, Suzanne and Mark tried to ground her for punishment, but Kay did not care. She was depressed all the time, but neither Kay nor anyone around her really knew it. They all went on with their lives and thought she was just an emotional kid dealing with all the adolescent ups and downs.

After barely getting by in tenth grade, she realized she would have to take an English class in order to return for her junior year at Kaysville High.
The following summer, Kay attended the required English class. There, for the first time in her life, she met a group of people that she actually felt comfortable with. They all had issues like Kay, they all hated school, and they were all there just waiting to get past it and to move on.

She was in a class of about fifteen and sat next to a boy named Sean. He and Kay had an instant connection from day one. They shared great banter and often teased each other. She felt comfortable with Sean and began hanging out with him after class. They spent a lot of time at Harvey's, a burger joint just down the road from Kaysville High, where they goofed off and flirted with each other for hours. Kay had never had a mutual connection with a boy before, and it was the first time she had butterflies. It was nice to be around someone who had the same feelings for her. They spent as much time as they could together. They were just friends at first, but it wasn't long before their unquestionable attraction and their teen hormones started to take over. Sean was crazy about Kay, and Kay loved everything about Sean. The only problem was that Sean was Mormon, and his family would not like the fact that he was dating anyone who was not a member, but they set that thought aside and carried on anyway.

After months of hanging out together, Sean decided it was time Kay met his parents. When Kay entered his old farmhouse that was set on fifty acres of land, the first thing his mother asked her was, "What Ward does your family belong to?"

Kay was taken off guard, but Sean covered for her. "She is in the fourth Ward," he fibbed.

His mother then began to drill Kay with questions about her family and their place within the church.

Sean again answered back, "Leave her alone."

Kay realized at that moment her being a non-Mormon was going to negatively affect her love life. She couldn't help but think back to the old bus and what her father made her promise. This was her first love, and for a moment she wished she could become Mormon if for no other reason than to fit in and be accepted by Sean's family. The problem was it had been engrained in her Mormons were cultists, and she should not get involved. She was learning it was a touchy subject and wanted to avoid it all costs.

It did not take long for Sean's mother to realize Kay was not Mormon, and she forbade Sean from seeing her, but Sean was like many other Mormon children. He did whatever he wanted, and Sean wanted to be with Kay all the time. It wasn't long before Kay and Sean were spending afternoons at her house instead of school. They missed many classes just to be alone. Sean had a truck, so they were able to come and go as they pleased. They had only a little money—just the two dollars a day that their parents gave them for lunch money—and it went straight into Sean's gas tank. Each day they talked about how they wanted to wait to "be together." Kay was not Mormon, but she took abstinence very seriously. They often kissed passionately for hours, and it was difficult for them to suppress their urges. After all, they were both sixteen, going on seventeen.

The days turned into weeks and then months. One rainy afternoon, they ditched school and decided they wanted to be together. They were committed to each other, and they knew nobody else would ever replace the love they were feeling. They made the decision to take it all the way. Sean did not care about his religion, and Kay was so caught up in what it felt like to be loved. She was completely consumed with Sean and completely vulnerable. She trusted their love for each other and believed Sean's commitment with all of her heart. He was so kind and caring, and he listened to her. For the first time, she felt adequate. Everyone knew they were in love, and it just made sense to them to take it to the next level.

Several months after they had consummated their relationship, Kay received the worst possible news: she was pregnant. They were still in love, but there were so many problems stemming from his family and their disapproval of the relationship. They had to hide their love and time together from his parents as it was, and now that she was pregnant, Kay didn't know what they were going to do.

She did not want to lose Sean, but she could feel how terrified he was. He loved her, but he was not ready to be a father, and he began pulling away from her. When he did, she would cry and tell him she needed him, but he just said he needed time to deal with what was happening. His religion started to overshadow all of the feelings he had for Kay.

After weeks of stress due to thoughts of losing Sean and him slowly disappearing from her life, she knew the only way to save their relationship would be to end the pregnancy. She was distraught and sick with fright at having to abort a child she knew she would love if she only had Sean's support. Kay had to make a difficult choice—Sean or their baby—and in the end, Sean convinced her to get an abortion.

She had scheduled the appointment and the procedure was set for the following day. She skipped school knowing she would be having the procedure done within twenty-four hours. Distraught and completely exhausted from no sleep, stress, and not eating, Kay collapsed on the bathroom floor and blacked out. She was out for hours until Luke came home from school and found her there. Luke called Suzanne at work, and she told him to call 911.

The ambulance rushed Kay to the hospital, where she was told she had lost the baby because her fragile body could not hold up to the consistent stress. She was only seventeen years old and had already lived the life of a forty-year-old. The doctor informed her she was anemic and that she was too weak to carry a child full term. After three months of pregnancy, she had to have a DNC, and she was sent home the next day.

News spread rapidly about Kay's hospital visit. Her friends and Sean immediately gathered around her. Sean was so ashamed at how he had behaved, yet he was relieved the whole saga was over and that he could move on without having to play Daddy just yet. Kay, however, was changed forever. She had once again been scarred for life. She was certain that now that the baby was out of the picture, albeit not in the way she'd planned, that she and Sean could resume their relationship from where they had left off, but Sean had other plans. He was too young to deal with his church's disapproval and his family's hatred of Kay, and all of the consequences, and he decided there was no place for Kay in his life. Baby or no baby, he was through with her.

Sean was the love of Kay's life, and no other boy would do. She was consumed with thoughts of him after their breakup, and she was disillusioned and in complete denial that their love could have ended so abruptly. He was her first, and she his, and she couldn't accept that he would move on and date another girl. She knew he still loved her and that he was only going to the Sadie Hawkins dance with Sharon because she was Mormon. He had to appease his Mormon mother, and anything he could do to draw attention away from the so-called "mistake" of being with Kay was his objective.

Kay had to learn that even though they were both involved in rebellious acts, to his family and hers, she was the only one to blame. Not only was she the bad,

65

uncontrollable child, but she was also the dirty, non-Mormon that had infected their clean LDS environment. He had done nothing wrong in their eyes. She struggled and battled with so many unanswered questions, one of them being, *Is Mormonism ruining my life, or was my father right? Maybe I am not worthy or beautiful enough to receive love.*

Her heart was broken. Sean was everything to her, her first and only love. She couldn't fathom being with another boy ever in her life. She had given herself to him—mind, body, and spirit—and they shared that moment of losing their virginity together. On top of that, her pain was acute, and she began to have reoccurring nightmares of the fateful night in her father's home. Sean had helped her blur out the thought of her father killing himself. He was her escape, and without him, she was just...just lost.

Kay was a lightweight when it came to drinking alcohol. One afternoon, she was drinking with some friends, and she broke down after several beers. Crying had become her new pastime. In a drunken, depressed stupor, she asked a couple of her friends to drive her past Sean's house, and as they passed it, she could see him working in the field next to his home. She begged them to stop the car, and reluctantly they did. She ran to him, sobbing, and clung onto him.

He wanted to hug her and be with her again, but after a few minutes, he started looking around to see if his family would see what was happening. "You need to get out of here and leave me alone," he said, pushing her off. "I will call you later."

She went home that evening, excitedly expecting his call and the rekindling of their love. As he promised, Sean did call, but he did not tell her what she wanted to hear. "I'm sorry," he said, "but you have to move on and let me go. It's not...it's not good for us to continue to see each other, Kay. It's just too difficult, and I'm getting so much flack from my family since you aren't Mormon. I can't...I just can't take the pressure. I'm sorry, and I love you, but I have to move on." He said he was doing his best to do so and told her she needed to stop driving by his house. He also let her know that after all that had taken place between them; he wanted to focus on church, family and possibility of going on mission after their senior year.

Even though she could not understand the complications of his religion and their relationship, Kay hung up the phone, certain that he loved her. Sean had been born and raised in Utah, so he was safe and protected in his world, his own little bubble, and his future was already planned out long before Kay even came along. She was a foreigner, and was not allowed to contaminate his clean cut image.

She was confused, lonely, and an outcast with a huge secret. She did not belong, and it was getting more difficult for her to function. It was much more difficult for her to move on than it was for Sean, for she had nobody to help her through. Once again, she sank into a deeper fantasy world.

She did not return to Kaysville High for her senior year. Instead, she chose to go to an alternative high school to get her GED. She could not fathom seeing Sean in the halls of school, especially if he was with another girl, which she was sure he would be because he was a catch. As far as Kay was concerned, high school was hell, and she had no desire to be in it anymore.

"Oh my God!" Lauren yelled out loud this time. She did not care if anyone heard. She was blown away and in complete shock. Once again, she realized her mother had kept one of the biggest secrets of her life hidden from her. Mom was pregnant when she was seventeen? She never got her diploma and only barely got her GED? What in the hell is this I'm reading? Who is this woman who calls herself my mother? She's been lying to me—to us— for all these years...

But then Lauren realized that her mother had not really lied at all. What she had done was withhold hurtful information to protect her. The only thing she'd lied about was her academic status, but even that was done in good intention: she only wanted to push and motivate Lauren to get the straight A's that she herself never had the opportunity to get. She would not accept anything less, and she demanded that her daughter do better than she had.

It was hard to believe, and what was more confusing was that her Grandma and Grandpa Kelley had never told Lauren about any of this. There were so many times that this information would have helped Lauren to understand her mother better. She was becoming angry and felt betrayed, but she still wanted to know more. She understood her mother was protecting her by keeping her past a secret, but there was no denying it was a lot to take in.

As she glanced down at the thick notebook, she realized she was only through a third of the way through it and then it dawned on her. I'm going to show up in this story somewhere! Her thoughts were racing, and she could not stop now. She wanted—no, she had—to know more. Lauren became queasy knowing eventually, her life with her mother would be coming up. At that moment, she wanted so badly for the whole book to be a lie.

8

Kay had spent well over a year trying to heal her wounds. She consumed herself with working at the mall and spending time watching her Jack Mormon friends party and go through heartbreaks and pregnancies of their own.

When Kay met Jesse, it was a completely different feeling than she had before with Justin and then with Sean. She was seventeen, almost eighteen, and had already been through her first heartbreak. She thought there was no way anything could hurt her as deeply as losing Sean.

She knew she did not want to date a Mormon boy again, and she would have to be open to a Jack Mormon whose families would accept her. She did not have any other options. Mormons reject any non-member and shun any family member that gets involved with one. It was like a secret war in Kay's life, subconscious and never discussed, but she had to accept that for what it was. Most of her Jack Mormon friends were allowed to hang out with anyone. If Kay was ever asked by them or their parents what religion she was, her answer would be "Christian," to which many of the Mormons and Jack Mormons responded with, "So are we." That would just confuse Kay even more, so she did her best to avoid discussing religion at all. It was very clear that Utah had little to offer a non-Mormon girl with no intention of being converted, she kept her promise, it wasn't because of her father's anymore, it was personal. After what had happened between her and Sean, she started to resent the religion.

It helped when Kay began hanging out with a bunch of rebellious girls from very Mormon families. They loved being wild, and boy did they party. Kay wasn't really the partying type, but it was an escape to sit back and watch the drama unfold. Each weekend, she drank a little and smoked cigarettes. She was entertained, and her preoccupation with the other kids helped her get over Sean and her life before him. The people she surrounded herself with lived to push the limit with their own families and had their own troubles, Kay just sat on the sidelines to watch the show.

The girls loved driving around looking for the guys they had crushes on. Several of Kay's wild friends had already had children. They rebelled by going out with bad boys and drinking. It was almost as if they were asking to get pregnant. Kay, on the other hand, had sworn off sex. She was too devastated by Sean to think about going there again. At the age of seventeen, her friend Melanie, who she called "Mel," had given birth to a beautiful baby girl named Mandy. Her friend Jeanie, who was sixteen, had a boy named Braden. Then there was Kendall, seventeen, who had given birth to a baby girl and had to give her up because her family would not allow her to keep it. All of them came from staunch Mormon families.

The girls were just blatantly defiant, except for Kay. It was amusing to her that she was the one who drank less and did not sleep around. She cared more about respecting her parents than all the girls combined. They had no boundaries because they had no idea what punishment felt like. They could yell at their parents, and unlike Kay's father would have, a hand would not be lifted against them. Even with all the abuse Kay had endured, she was completely mortified by those parents allowing their kids to walk all over them. They just calmly asked their daughters, in the midst of them cussing them out, to stay home for family night on Wednesday evenings, to which the raging, ungrateful young women would yell, "Shut up," "Go to hell," "Screw you!" or "I am not hanging around here. I hate you." Those were just some of the phrases Kay heard them use with their parents. She had no idea what family night was about, but knew that the girls all hated it. Kay just figured the lack of punishment was due to their parents being too tired to respond, because

70

they had too many children. They only seemed to care when something really bad happened, like pregnancy, an accident or something that could cause them to be excommunicated from the church.

After months of hanging out with her rebellious friends and being distracted from her pain, she met Jesse. The girls had gotten together on a Friday night to cruise the boulevard and ran into him and some of his friends. Kay was instantly attracted to his calm demeanor. Little did she know he wasn't as calm as he was stoned. He had piercing blue eyes that looked as if someone had placed light blue marbles in his eye sockets. She was mesmerized by his stare, even though his eyes were really just glassed over from the pot he'd smoked a half-hour before they met. He had medium brown hair with blond highlights. He was pretty short for a guy, only five-eight, but she liked him right away. They ended up sitting in his truck talking till three in the morning and then making out until six.

Jesse seemed so sweet, and he had a great job working for the railway. He drove cars off the train and parked them on trucks that would then drive them to car dealerships in the area.

They had become so close and spent most of their free time together; it was no surprise when she finally caved in and gave up on her no sex rule.

They spent hours upon hours in his mother's home, where he had a room in the basement. It was all very romantic to Kay, as she had never had a normal relationship.

After several months, Kay basically moved in to Jesse's room, and the two seemed happy together. She noticed he had a temper and that he smoked a lot of weed, as well as dabbled in other drugs. However, for Kay, it was better than being rejected by someone who thought they were better than her. At that time, she smoked cigarettes quite frequently and had a beer every now and again, but never got involved with using drugs, they didn't' interest her.

71

Jesse did not treat his mother well because he said she drove him crazy. Even though he mouthed off to her and called her names, she always did whatever Jesse wanted and took care of him. His father had passed away years earlier from a heart attack His mother claimed to be Mormon but she did not attend church, which probably didn't go well with her prescription drug habit; she smoked and popped pills like they were candy. Jesse and his family were considered Jack Mormons since they never attended church. Jesse's grandparents, on the other hand, were staunch Mormons. They attended services every Sunday and had followed all the necessary procedures and practices Mormons must undertake in order to marry and enter the temple.

There were only a handful of people Kay knew who actually admitted to being Jack Mormons, people who had learned it was not for them and who had no intention of practicing the religion. Kay understood at age seventeen that it would be difficult for them to know anything different. She knew they were born into an area that was saturated with everything Mormon. However, it was different for her. She had not always lived in Utah, and she knew there were other places in the world—Ohio, for one—where Mormonism did not invade every facet of life. She could not express this knowledge to anyone, though, because nobody cared and nobody would listen. She was living inside the bubble, and she kept her thoughts and her past to herself.

Jesse worked the swing shift for the railroad, and for a nineteen-year-old he was making good money. One night he was walking back to the train after parking a car, when suddenly, out of nowhere, came a man with a sledgehammer. The man whacked Jesse with it, knocking him out cold and breaking his jaw.

The following day, Kay received a phone call from Jesse's mother telling her that Jesse was in the hospital. Kay and his mother went to visit him, but when they got there, he could not talk. He was drugged up and mad as hell. Kay had only been dating him for a few months, and she had accepted that he smoked pot daily and drank and used cocaine once in a while. She knew having his mouth wired shut for months was going to mean months of stress for her boyfriend and for her.

The worst part was that Jesse was also fired from his job. Through his wired mouth, Jesse explained to Kay what happened. Apparently, Jesse and his attacker, a co-worker, had had words with each other. After that, the man had made it his mission to beat the hell out of Jesse, even if it meant getting himself and Jesse fired in the process. He wanted to make sure he paid Jesse back for whatever it was he was stupid enough to say.

Kay believed his story and continued to find comfort with him, even though he was turning out to be nothing but trouble. His deviant ways were not something Kay seemed to be concerned with. After all, her life had been so much more tumultuous than a man with a temper who used drugs. He seemed to love Kay, and that was all that mattered to her. She craved love and would take it no matter what package it came in.

Even though Jesse's mouth was wired shut, it did not stop him from using drugs and drinking. If anything, it only fueled the fire. He began to treat Kay horribly, due to his own misery or his drug and alcohol use or both.

One night they attended a party at the home of one of Kay's girlfriend's. Jesse had been drinking and using drugs excessively throughout the day and after several more hours of saturating his liver with alcohol he needed to throw up. Immediately, everyone stopped what they were doing and began looking for wire cutters. It was just a matter of time before Jesse's body was going to violently reject all of the junk he'd been stuffing up his nose and down his throat. People were frantic and running around the house trying to find some sort of tool to cut the wires away from his teeth or he would choke on his own vomit and die. Jesse didn't want to be taken to the hospital because they knew he'd be arrested for drug use, among other things. Someone had a tool kit in their truck and pulled out a pair of pliers. Some of his friends began working on cutting through each wire until his mouth was completely open, just in time for Jesse to throw up what seemed to be a gallon of alcohol.

* * *

Because Jesse was not working, he began dealing drugs as well as using them. He dealt methamphetamine, otherwise known as crack, similar to cocaine but cheaper. Kay did not care. She was in love with the crack head. She could not see straight, and in her oblivious state, she just wanted to feel accepted, no matter the circumstance—at least up until they got an apartment together.

Once they were in their own place, Jesse became obsessed with dealing. He had purchased a scale, and he had become so paranoid that he wouldn't let Kay walk around apartment because he was afraid she might throw off the drug scale. One evening, Jesse said he needed to use Kay's car to make a drug run. When she refused, Jesse threw her to the ground and started choking her, yelling, "Fuck you, bitch! I will kill you!" She lay on the floor grasping for air, and before she knew it, he had taken her keys and driven away in her car. That moment sent her reeling back to reality and she needed to get away from him before he hurt her again like her father had.

Kay was finally done with Jesse and his life style. He had crossed the line with her and there was no going back. When he returned, she was packing her things to move out. In his anger, he began helping her by throwing her belongings out over the balcony of the apartment, screaming, "Get the fuck out then, you fucking bitch! Get out of here! I hate you!"

She moved back in with Mark and Suzanne. She never told anyone about it, but all this time she kept having nightmares, reliving in her dreams the night her father killed himself. Kay hoped for a fresh start after she left Jesse, and she took a job at Denny's as a waitress.

* * *

Several weeks into waiting tables and bringing people their Grand Slams for tips, she realized it was not a career she wanted to have for her whole life. She signed up for a computer course that would award her a certificate, and she hoped it would lead to an office job. For the first time, she had her own plans to work toward and was focused on work and school. It was the first time she actually felt good about herself.

A month passed, and Kay received a call from an old co-worker she had worked with at a t-shirt store part time at the mall. It had been almost two years since she had seen or spoken to Lori, so the call came as a total surprise. Kay was making progress with her life and had even quit hanging around her old friends, who were still partying. She was open for new people in her life, and the last time she had seen Lori, she was attending college.

Lori always seemed to have a good life, and her family was wealthy. She was not Mormon, a drinker, a smoker, or a druggie, and she just happened to be from Ohio. So, Kay felt karma had something to do with Lori calling her out of the blue; the call came at just at the right time. Kay needed someone like Lori to help get over the damage that Jesse, the drug-dealing scum, had done to her already fragile self-esteem.

Kay had just turned twenty and was blossoming. She was still as thin as a rail, but her dark hair was getting long. Her skin was pail, but it made her green eyes stand out like emeralds. She had a big, beautiful smile, perfectly sculpted by years in braces.

For two months, Lori and Kay spent every moment of their free time working out together. They both loved swimming and at Lori's apartment complex in Ogden. Lori was a beautiful, strong, confident person, and the two of them just clicked. They discussed what kind of dreams and aspirations they had, and for the first time in Kay's life, she felt promise for a bright future. Lori inspired Kay, unlike her old friends who were focused on drinking and partying. She started to realize she could have more and live outside of the small world she had been a prisoner of.

Kay completed her computer course and looked forward to quitting her waitress job at Denny's. Within a couple weeks of receiving her certificate, she started working as a receptionist for a sheet metal fabrication company and was on cloud nine.

In the meantime, Lori had become an assistant manager at the same store where they had met and worked together several years prior.

Lori lived with her boyfriend Ben. He was a good guy that came from a family with strong Mormon ties. His father had two wives and two families, and he watched his mother struggle to make ends meet because his father could not support both large families. Ben had sworn he would never allow his life to turn out the same way as his parents', so he was always at work or at school, busy earning his degree in biology. He was a good catch, a tall, dark, and handsome guy with a very dry sense of humor. Lori and he made an attractive couple, even though they argued a lot, when Ben was home.

* * *

Kay and Lori had quickly become best friends, and it came as a complete and total shock to both of them to find out that Kay had been pregnant with Jesse's baby for the past three months. They sat huddled on the bathroom floor together, staring at the second pregnancy test, which confirmed what the first test had already told them. Kay looked at Lori and said, "I need to take one more. I just don't believe it!"

Lori looked Kay in the eyes and said, "No, Kay. You really are pregnant." She wrapped her arms around Kay, and they began crying together.

Kay was devastated. She finally had her life going in a positive direction; only to find out she was pregnant. It was like a time bomb ticking away in her womb, threatening to explode her future into shrapnel. She just kept repeating the words, "Why now? Why now?"

Several months prior to Lori and Kay reconnecting, Lori had had an abortion while pregnant with Ben's baby, so she was still dealing with the pain of her decision and carried a lot of regret. She knew firsthand what it felt like to make the big decision Kay was going to have to face and was there to support her friend either way. Kay knew she would not be able to live with abortion yet again, but she also knew she was not ready to be a mom. Still, given her options and the fact that Lori would be there to support her, she was excited about the idea of going through the pregnancy. It was as if Lori and Kay were having a baby together.

Kay wondered why she even bothered to tell Jesse she was pregnant. He was so strung out on drugs, he couldn't comprehend that he had actually impregnated Kay. Jesse had not heard from her in months and was still dealing drugs for an income. He let Kay know that he did not want her to get an abortion, but he wasn't prepared to take care of a baby.

After all the loss, pain, and loneliness she had experienced in her life, she believed a baby would at least provide her with some kind of security; the baby would always be someone to love her and someone for her to love. To Kay, abortion was out of the question. She knew she couldn't live with a decision like that—not again. Besides that, it seemed as if everyone was getting married in Utah because men had returned from their missions and were ready to marry and start their own families. Kay, now twenty years old, had actually waited to have a child among her old crowd of friends. She was the only one left who had not actually delivered a child, and now she was going to catch up with them.

Lori and Kay were committed to the pregnancy and made the best of it. They went shopping together, and Lori helped Kay pick out the crib, car seat, and stroller. Everything was so meticulously planned out; it had to be right down to the dime, for there was very little money. Once people at work found out Kay was pregnant and unmarried, they made up an excuse to terminate her. Her manager used the exact words, "I just don't think you are a good fit for the company. It is just a gut feeling." Kay was humiliated and under a tremendous amount of stress. She was living with her parents and wanted to be able to work to support herself and the baby. She wanted nothing to do with Jesse and expected nothing from him. This was her baby and hers alone.

For the last few months of Kay's pregnancy, she took her mother's advice and drew unemployment, expecting to find a job once the baby was born. Her pregnancy went well, with no complications, and she and Lori spent hours thinking of names and shopping. Lori had money and did not hold back when it came to buying Kay whatever she needed. She loved Kay like a sister and could not wait to be there for her in delivery, and even after the baby was born. They had found out together that the baby was a girl, even though Kay said she knew all along.

Kay gave birth to an eight-pound, four-ounce baby girl. Everyone who saw her agreed she was a beautiful baby. She had a full head of dark hair, which shocked Kay when she first saw her since she had always assumed her baby would be bald like she was when she was born.

Lori had been such a good friend to her through thick and thin and Kay wanted to surprise her, so when the nurse finally laid the baby in Kay's arms, she looked up at Lori and said, "I am naming her Lauren, after you."

Lori, with tears in her eyes, gave Kay a hug. She was honored, for not only was she able to see the birth of Kay's baby, but the baby would also bear her name.

Ben had come up to meet Lori at the hospital and wanted to see baby Lauren. He walked into the room and immediately fell in love with the infant. She was so beautiful, and he was in awe of her perfect round face and full head of black hair.

Lori and Ben went home after that, and Kay fell asleep. She woke at four in the morning and asked a nurse to put the baby in her arms. As she looked down at Lauren sleeping, so little and precious, she was moved to tears. She was looking at the person who she would finally have to spend the rest of her life with. It was going to be her and Lauren against the world. She knew she could raise her better than she had been raised, and she would make sure to tell her every day how loved and beautiful she was.

The next day, while she was still in the hospital, some friends and family stopped by to see her, but she had one surprise that she never expected. When Sean walked into her hospital room, she almost passed out. He looked at her holding Lauren and said, "You look so beautiful." Kay was teary eyed, and the fact of the matter was, he still gave her butterflies, even though it had been almost four years. Sean asked if he could hold Lauren, and Kay handed the baby to him. As he sat in the chair next to Kay's bed and stared down at the baby with her thick head of raven-black hair. He looked at Kay with tears in his eyes said, "This would have been our baby."

Kay did not know how to feel about that. She had so many emotions coursing through her, and the last thing she expected was for Sean to literally walk into her life at the most inappropriate time.

He then said, "You know, I would have married you if things could have been different." Sean had not gone on the mission after high school. He had moved into a home on his family's land and helped them with the farm. He really did love Kay, but he gave her up because

79

of family and religion. Sean hated Jesse and knew he was bad news. He kept up through friends on where Kay was and who she was seeing because he worried about her, especially when he found out she was falling for a known drug dealer. He loved her no matter what his parents or anyone said, and he knew she would always be the love of his life, but he was too young and weak to do anything about it.

With Lauren's birth, Kay had a new love. She finally had someone who would not walk away because of religion or abuse her in any way. She had everything she needed with baby Lauren. Kay would always love Sean, but seeing him again—looking at him holding Lauren— just didn't feel right. It had taken her years to heal her heart and move on after their breakup. She loved him and always would, but she could not believe he had come to see her. She wanted and needed to start over and leave the past behind her so she could focus on baby Lauren. Kay asked him nicely to leave. He was hurt but understood and respected her request, tenderly kissed her on the forehead and left.

When Lauren finished reading about the events that occurred before and after she was born, she was overwhelmed. She had never wanted to accept it before and had always been in denial, but facts were facts, and now she knew the truth. Her father was a total loser.

She yawned and was torn about whether to keep reading or not. She knew the stories that followed were going reveal her mother's real feelings, her secret insights, about their life together. She felt it would be much more difficult to read about them, now knowing her mother's horrific childhood, but she read on.

9

Kay was basking in her new bundle of joy. Never for one moment did she have any idea what was about to happen next. She knew Jesse was not interested in the baby, and that was just fine with her, but Jesse's family had no intention of allowing Kay to stop them from having a relationship with Lauren. Even though Kay continually reassured them she was fine with them being involved in Lauren's life, it just wasn't enough proof for them. They wanted Jesse to get involved and pushed him into seeing Lauren. It was at that point that Kay realized her allowing them to be a part of her life was about to backfire.

Kay was still in the hospital when Jesse's grandmother called Kay to let her know she felt Jesse had a right to see his child and that he would be coming to the hospital. Kay started crying and asked her, "Why are you doing this to me now?" Kay explained to her that he wanted nothing to do with the baby during the pregnancy, and she couldn't understand why he was so interested now. His family believed Kay had ruined the relationship between them and that she should give him a second, third, and tenth chance. Kay had not talked to him for months and had no intention of talking to him ever again. It was her plan to raise Lauren on her own, period. She had endured nine months of pregnancy on her own, and she had had purchased with hard work and creative thinking all of the things the baby would need. She did not need trouble; she just wanted peace.

But Jesse's family was relentless, very religious, and oblivious to the fact Jesse was a liar and a drug-dealing loser who just used them for money. They treated him as if he was still two years old, and they convinced him he needed to see his child and be involved in his child's life. This just so happened to be at a time when he needed money, so he did whatever they said. He had no intention of supporting Lauren or Kay. For him, it was all about making sure his grandma was happy so she would keep dishing out the dough and eventually leave him her inheritance.

Jesse's family felt Kay was trouble in the. After all, she was not one of them, a Mormon. They seriously believed she had Lauren in order to trap Jesse, when in fact; Kay wanted nothing to do with him. For her, it was a twist of fate that she had gotten pregnant when she did, but they would not believe a word she told them.

Kay had been through so much that she was tired and unable to fight with Jesse's persistent and demanding grandmother. She had no control while she was stuck lying in the hospital. Her mother had left to go take care of things at home, and she was in the room alone when suddenly there was a man peeking around the corner. It was Jesse! He walked in with three people in tow, his entourage of drug-dealing, trouble-making friends. They all reeked of smoke. Kay had quit smoking when she found out she was pregnant, and the stench made her very ill—almost as ill as seeing Jesse and his gross buddies in the first place.

When they walked in, Kay was propped up in bed, holding the baby. Her eyes breathed a fire of hate as she looked at him with disgust.

Jesse walked over to the bed, looked down at his daughter Lauren, and said, "She's cute." He then looked at Kay, who was pissed off beyond belief and couldn't believe the son of a bitch had the gall to stand next to her. Suddenly he said, "If you're going to act like this, then I am going to just leave!"

Kay roared back in a fierce voice, "Well there's the fucking door. Get the hell out of here!"

His entourage was stunned. They had known Kay for years, and that kind of anger and strength was out of character for her.

Jesse knew she meant every word she said, and he immediately looked over to his buddies and asked them to step out for a few minutes. Jesse then said, "You know, this is entirely your fault. You do not want me to be a part of her life, even though I've tried."

Kay howled back, "Get the fuck out of here!"

Without any hesitation Jesse conjured up some tears, pretending he was shocked and could not believe this woman, who had been so in love with him, wanted absolutely nothing to do with him.

All Kay wanted was to enjoy this time. She was finally able to see and be with her baby, and Jesse was ruining everything by stinking up the room with the dirty smell of secondhand smoke, lies, and more bullshit. He just would not leave. He continued with his tears, saying he was sorry and wanted to be there for her and Lauren. He said he was going to make changes. As he went on and on, Kay kept repeating the words, "Leave! Leave now!" but no matter how many times she told him to "Get the hell out!" he kept on using his words to manipulate Kay. She was exhausted not only from giving birth, but from being a rock for the last six months. She had forgotten all of the feelings she had for him because she had to.

Suzanne and Mark then walked into the room. When they saw Jesse there and Kay in tears, Mark immediately said in an angry voice, "Kay, is everything okay in here?"

Jesse started babbling and quickly said, "I have to go, but I will be back later, okay?"

Kay did not respond.

Suzanne was fuming and in complete shock. "What was he doing here? What is going on?"

Kay then explained how Jesse's grandmother had called and that it was her pressure that caused Jesse to feel the need to visit.

Suzanne was furious and went on and on about it. "He has a lot of nerve," she said, along with calling him a weasel and a coward for bringing his friends with him.

Finally Kay said, "Mom, it's over! Now let's just enjoy baby."

A couple hours passed, and Kay had many visitors. One was Lori. When she heard Jesse had been there, she was livid. Nothing worried Lori more than to have him come back into Kay's life. She had spent months with Kay, and she knew the girl had come a long way since that miserable relationship. She had built up so much self-esteem after all she had gone through. Kay had made a promise to herself and to everyone that she wanted nothing to do with Jesse, and she meant it. The last thing she ever expected was to see him crying at her bedside asking to be a part of hers and Lauren's lives. Kay was on so much medication for the pain she had endured delivering an eight-pound baby, and she was barely able to comprehend anything. She began to think Jesse's visit was just some bad painkiller-induced dream.

Seeing Jesse and his desperation to make amends and be there for his child, telling Kay he really did love her, was hard for her. She hated the fact that he had left her pregnant and alone while he was out and about doing drugs and partying. When she had first met Jesse, he had discussed becoming an architect. He was an incredible artist, even when he was just doodling. He had potential, and Kay believed him until she was attacked by him due to the drugs.

Kay had so much to think about. She and Lori had been so wrapped up in her pregnancy she had forgotten that Lori would be moving away. She had plans to leave Utah within the three or four months. Lori and Ben were getting married. He had finished getting his degree and joined the Army. Ben would be stationed somewhere on the East Coast once he finished boot camp. Kay knew she would be left alone and would miss Lori terribly.

Kay took Lauren home from the hospital to live with Suzanne and Mark until she could get her own place. That meant getting a job right away. She was ready to get to work and make some money of her own. She had been relying on food stamps, petty unemployment checks, and occasional help from Lori to get by while she was pregnant. Mark and Suzanne did not have extra money, because Mark had been laid off from his job six months earlier and money was tight. It was going to be a struggle, but Kay knew she would figure it out somehow.

Jesse had become persistent about asking if he could come and see the baby, but all he really wanted was to get back with Kay. He realized he loved her, but only when she truly wanted nothing to do with him. She had become a challenge for him.

* * *

Suzanne was disgusted, and Lori detested him. They knew he was coming around and breaking Kay down little by little. Kay was doing her best to focus on Lauren and finding a job. It had only been weeks since she'd given birth, and Jesse was pushing to get back together with her. It all felt strange to Kay. She was experiencing post-partum depression and could not help but be edgy and easily annoyed. She could not think clearly, and her life had changed so much and the responsibility of being a mother was hitting her.

It was hard work, and the baby kept her up at night, which just added more to an already stressful time. She finally told Jesse to back off and leave her alone. He agreed, but within hours, he returned begging for her to see him. She agreed reluctantly and felt forced to listen to what he had to say. He took her into her bedroom, and while giving her a speech about how he had every intention of getting a job and supporting her and the baby, he got down on one knee and pulled out a ring. Kay went into instant shock. It did not seem like it was really happening. Every single one of her plans for raising Lauren on her own went right out the window. She had become so good at forgetting, and this time was no exception. She had many questions, and the first one was, "Where did you get the money to buy this ring?"

He let her know he used his rent money and told her he was planning on moving out of the apartment he was sharing with several other guys and would to go live with his grandma. He said he was hoping that somehow they could get a place together.

Kay was dumfounded and asked, "Just exactly how are you going to afford to get us a place?"

He said, "Well, I'm going to get a job as soon as possible, and then we can move."

She was so confused. She wore a blank stare as he continued his nonsensical conversation about how he was miraculously going to be able to support her and their baby. It was all too good to be true, but Kay could not help but want to believe him.

When she told her mother and Mark the news and showed them the ring, Suzanne immediately let out a sigh of disgust. "How can you believe him, Kay? And why would you want to now?"

When Lori found out the news, she was furious and could not believe Kay would be so foolish as to believe Jesse was capable of telling the truth. To everyone but Kay, Jesse's mother, and his grandmother, Jesse was a loser, a liar, and a scam artist.

* * *

Several months passed, and Kay and Lori grew apart. They had been inseparable for almost a year, and suddenly they were barely talking. Kay was busy taking care of Lauren and looking for work and Lori was planning her move and wedding to Ben, who had been transferred to Fort Meade in Maryland. Lori and Kay got together and said their bittersweet goodbyes. Lori was upset with Kay and felt she had made a huge mistake for allowing Jesse into her life again. Kay understood but was hoped she was wrong. They vowed, no matter what, to stay in contact forever.

Kay and Jesse moved into Suzanne and Mark's basement, which was a small apartment. Kay found a job working the swing shift on an assembly line for a medical supply company. It was a crappy job, but it paid well and offered good benefits. Jesse found a part-time job working at a convenience store, and he watched Lauren in the evenings while Kay worked.

She was always tired, but things were rolling along. She knew Jesse hated his job as much, if not more than she hated hers. He let her know one evening after she returned home from work that he was fired. He gave her a lame excuse that he was let go because someone was caught stealing on his shift. He made sure to tell her it wasn't his fault and eased Kay's mind by letting her know he was interviewing the next day for a better job as a welder.

Jesse interviewed the next day, and the company hired him. They wanted him to start as soon as he passed a drug test the following morning. When Kay came home from work the evening before the scheduled drug test to find him smoking a joint, she went ballistic. She was exhausted and carrying the weight for all three of them, and there he was ruining any chance of passing that drug test so he could pitch in and do his part again. She began yelling at him, and he punched a hole in the wall. When she tried to walk away from him, he grabbed her and pushed her to the ground. She started screaming at him, "Get the hell out!"

Mark overheard and came downstairs and told Jesse the same thing Kay had told him: "Get the hell out of our house."

Then that all hell broke loose. Jesse punched Mark, and the fight was on. Suzanne called the police, but by the time they arrived, Jesse was gone, once again leaving a mess in his wake.

Lauren was only six months old, but Kay was through with Jesse and wanted to ban him from seeing the baby, even if he was her biological father. Jesse had told his family a completely different story, and his tall tale prompted them to pay for an attorney so he could try for visitation and full custody of Lauren. Jesse was an excellent liar he led his family to believe that he had been beaten up by Kay's father, who he said was a drug addict.

For months, Kay had that same reoccurring nightmare. It seemed as if she would never be able to shake the horror of seeing her father's head blown apart, and it only got worse when there was stress in her life, which Jesse had handed her plenty of.

In light of the false rumors Jesse had told them about Mark, Jesse's family fought for him to have full custody of Lauren. It was his word against Kay's. Not only had he come back into her life and caused hell, but he was trying to take her baby away from her. He was sick and his lies were never ending. He never had any intention of getting and keeping a regular job. He just wanted to freeload off of others.

It took months of court battles before Kay was granted full custody of Lauren, but in the process, the truth about Jesse finally came out. During the course of the all the depositions, testimonies, litigations, and accusations, Jesse was arrested for drunk driving and possession of marijuana. That stopped the custody battle, along with all the complete nonsense he had created and his false stories about Mark. But Lauren was already one year old, and he had made it a difficult one. Kay had been so busy working and fighting with Jesse; she didn't have the time she had dreamt of to spend bonding with her baby.

* * *

Kay wanted to move on. Work seemed to become more important than everything, she had to support Lauren and that was all that mattered. She was moving up the

89

chain at her job, even after only a year of working on an assembly line. She applied for a receptionist position, and she got the job. She was relieved, and it was a nice feeling to be able to dress up every day. Finally, she'd landed the job—the one she'd wanted to do ever since she had received the computer course certificate.

Jesse moved on and moved in with a woman to whom he was engaged within weeks. Her family threw them a huge wedding, and he did not bother inviting Lauren. Kay was fine with that. What she wasn't fine with was that everywhere she went, in town or even at work, people would approach her and call her bitch because Jesse had told everyone that Kay would not allow Lauren to come to his wedding. It seemed no matter how hard Kay tried to escape the psycho; he was dead set on finding new ways to harass her.

Jesse's Grandmother called her one day to apologize for everything her and her family had put her through. She let Kay know Jesse was cut off from her support and not allowed in her home. She hoped someday he would become responsible and turn his life around. She begged Kay to forgive her and to allow her to spend time with Lauren. Kay being so good at forgetting agreed to let her watch Lauren in the evening. Kay needed money. It was becoming hard to get by financially. So at night Kay waited tables at a sports bar in Ogden. It seemed as though everyone had more time with Lauren than she had.

* * *

Kay found had an apartment for her and Lauren in Riverdale, fifteen miles north of where she had lived with Mark and Suzanne.

In spite of her bad luck with men, over the next three years Kay dated a little, they always ended up being players. Kay just wanted to fall in love and be loved by someone, anyone. Lauren seemed to want to be with Mark,

90

Suzanne and Jesse's Grandmother more than her, and Kay began to feel lonely.

Reading all of this, Lauren was sad. She had never realized how lonely her mother must have felt. She remembered times when her mother had worked two jobs. Kay would come home so tired and break down and cry because there wasn't enough money to pay rent or buy food. Lauren recalled that her father did not pay child support, and no matter how hard Kay fought to make him pay, he simply refused; Jesse loved the fact Kay had to struggle. Lauren suddenly had a feeling of resentment for her father and wanted so badly to give her mother a hug.

As the flight continued its course over the Atlantic, Lauren kept reading, wondering what other secrets lurked in her mother's past and in her heart.

10

After three years at Denmark, Kay grew tired of answering phones. She had had enough of being locked up in a box she knew she was not built that way. She had to be able to move around and have freedom, from her desk. She often witnessed one salesperson after the other walk through the doors of Demark. They would walk in say, "I am here to see so-and-so," sign in, meet with so and so, and then be on their way. She had heard they made good money.

Wow! What a life! She thought, envying them. *If only I could do that. I wonder how I could get into sales. Do I need a degree?* She decided to start asking every sales representative that walked in to meet with a manager how they got their job and what qualifications were needed.

One day she asked Don, a salesman that came in quite often to meet with the purchasing manager. He handed her a business card of a recruiter in Salt Lake City and said, "Call this lady. She can help you. She helped me years ago. Good luck, kid."

Kay contacted Diane at Shelling Personnel. She asked Kay to fax over her resume and told her she would call her. Kay had a strong resume since she had been with Demark for almost five years, and as soon as Diane had reviewed it, she called Kay to set up an interview.

Shelling Personnel was in Salt Lake City, a forty-mile drive one way. She took a day off of work and drove into the city to meet with Diane. Pat, the owner of Shelling, joined the interview and asked Kay if she had ever sold anything before.

Kay told her, "No, but I know I could, if given the chance."

Pat told Kay, "It's a risk to hire you, but I see something in you. You have the potential to make good money, but starting out, you must be willing to take a risk and work for straight commission."

Kay knew it was risky but she had grown so much over the past five years, she had built up a confidence that she had never had before. She knew it would be difficult, but so was working two jobs. She was ready for a challenge. So, she gave up security to go after her dream.

She worked in the center of downtown Salt Lake City, and it was surprising to her how quickly she adjusted. She felt like she was moving up in the world, and she wanted to make as much money as possible and get as far away from her past as possible. This was just the baby step she needed to make it happen.

As it turned out, Pat's intuition about her was right. Kay was a natural, placing people in jobs within the first several weeks. She had her very own office and freedom. She was used to a rigid schedule, as that had been drilled into her for the past five years. Kay was there from eight to five every day, and Pat loved her for it. The other women in the office were envious of Kay because she was younger, and did her job well.

Her office was on the eighth floor of high-rise building. Kay had picked up smoking again several years prior and whenever she or any of the other employees needed to take a smoke break, they had to go down to the parking garage. So she would take a break daily around ten o'clock in the morning and take the elevator down for her morning cigarette.

A certain man pulled into his parking space, the first space by the elevator, each day around the same time, and she always thought to herself, *Great. There he is again, and he always stares at me. It's so uncomfortable.* He was an older man, maybe thirty years older than her. He looked very professional and distinguished. He had several cars, and one just happened to be a 1960 Mercedes convertible. Kay thought he was trying too hard to be cool, and he had an arrogance about him that repulsed her.

One morning he got off the elevator and told Kay he was flying off to Chicago to see the Bulls play. Immediately Kay replied, "Good for you" before she put out her cigarette and proceeded to the elevator. Then, there was a period of what seemed to be months when she did not see him.

Then one morning he pulled into the parking garage and when he got out of his car he seemed preoccupied. Kay thought she would throw him off guard and asked "How was the Bulls game."

He looked puzzled and after a few moments responded with, "Oh, I ended up not going. I flew to Cabo San Lucas with my friends and went deep sea fishing."

Kay was now caught off guard because she and several of her old friends from Denmark had just purchased tickets to go to Cabo. They were leaving in six weeks. She was so excited to go on her first real vacation, and it seemed to be a huge coincidence that he had brought up that location. She immediately told him about her upcoming trip to Cabo. He was more than happy to see that the woman whom he had been staring down for months was actually engaging in conversation with him. He opened up his wallet, handed her his business card, and told her his name was Richard. He also mentioned that if she was interested in seeing pictures of his friend's yacht and Cabo, she should contact him. She was immediately taken aback by such a suggestion, but she thanked him and glanced at his business card, which read "Greystone Petroleum."

* * *

Kay had been with Shelling for a little over a year. Once again she craved freedom. She was growing tired of sitting in an office each day, and her dream of becoming an outside sales representative was becoming more of a

95

long shot than a reality. She was doing well at being an employment recruiter and earned almost double what she had while working two jobs. She began looking for new opportunities, but once again she was having a hard time because she did not have a degree. She had tried going to school while working and raising Lauren on her own, but it became too overwhelming.

She was also growing tired of commuting forty miles each way to and from work. One morning while at a standstill on the freeway heading into work, she looked up and noticed a Greystone Petroleum truck in front of her. She immediately thought, *Oh my God! I know the guy who works for them. I wonder if I could get a job working as a sales representative for them.* She could not wait to get into the office and find his business card to give him a call. She had been so bugged by him for months, but she really wanted to be in outside sales and was willing to ask anyone for an opportunity.

Back in the office, she found his card and discovered his name was Richard Greystone. Under his name was his title, "President." She was stunned, and she thought this could really be her chance. She knew he liked her, and he had told her to call him. All she had to do was ask and maybe her dream would really come true. She called his office, and they let her know he was out of town for the next week. They offered to leave him a message, but she declined.

After the week passed, she called his office again. The receptionist asked who was calling, and Kay immediately said without thinking, "Just a friend."

She was put on hold, and within a few moments, an annoyed man abruptly asked, "Who is this?"

She calmly replied. "The smoker."

Suddenly she heard, "What? Who? Oh my God! Well, hello there! How are you? What can I do for you?"

Kay let him know she had tried to reach him the week prior and then, without beating around the bush, she asked him if he was hiring sales representatives. He asked

96

her if she had experience with the petroleum industry. She let him know she was a quick learner and would be able to pick up the business lingo if given the opportunity.

"Tell you what," he said. "Let's go to lunch and talk."

So several days later they met in the infamous garage. He drove her to lunch at Biatti's, a four-star Italian restaurant. They had a great conversation. He was easy to talk to, and Kay was beginning to think he was a nice man and that maybe she had been wrong about him. She thought for a few minutes that she might actually have a shot at working for him, but then he said, "I am not hiring a sales representative. I am looking for a travel companion."

Kay was mortified when she discovered all he was looking for was an escort—a prostitute. She was disgusted and made it clear there was no way in hell that was going to happen. She also demanded he take her back to her office.

He could tell he had hit a nerve with her, and he quickly paid the check before they headed back to work.

Several hours later, he called her. Now she was the one who was annoyed when answering his call. He apologized and let her know he would be interested in her handling all of Greystone's hiring. He said he would let his Human Resources Department know that they were to work with her and only her to find candidates for all job openings. Needless to say, Kay was more than obliged and was not about to say no. It was a great opportunity to make some good money, and since she worked for straight commission, he had won her over. Pat was thrilled to hear the news, but Kay knew there had to be a catch.

He called the next day and invited her to a Jazz game at the Delta Center. He told her he had season tickets and that the person who was supposed to go could not make it. He said he immediately thought of her because she might like to see a game since she had only seen professional basketball games on television. He knew how to play it cool. After all, he had been womanizing for more than forty years and was an expert. Kay felt obligated and excited to go to see the Jazz play. She agreed, and they met at the Delta Center, where he had courtside seats for her first NBA game, the Jazz against the San Antonio Spurs.

It was unexpected, but he mentioned he had daughters that were two years apart and born on the same day. Kay asked when their birthdates were, and when he said "August 31," she yelled out, "Mine too!" He was shocked and surprised.

They left the game during halftime and went to the New Yorker where he bought her dinner. They talked for hours, and she was so surprised at how comfortable she felt. She had mixed feelings and uncomfortable moments as she thought about the fact that the man was three decades her senior. Nevertheless, she enjoyed his company and the evening so much that she put the age thing aside and decided to take advantage of being treated like a lady for once.

The following week, he asked her to lunch again, and she accepted his invitation. This time, he had brought some other young women with him. They were in their thirties, they loved hanging out with him, and he always paid for everything. Kay was realizing he wasn't a bad guy and he was a lot of fun to be around. Some of the women had gone with him when he traveled with his friends, and it was supposedly purely platonic. One lunch turned into two dinners and then several parties at his penthouse. Kay was starting to get a taste of the good life. She was seeing a world that was so far from her old life, and she never wanted to look back. She just wanted to keep moving forward.

* * *

Kay and four of her girlfriends flew to Cabo San Lucas and had the best week of their lives. It was an exciting time for her, as she had never been to coast or seen the ocean, and she absolutely loved it. She knew that someday she wanted to live near the water. She did not know how, when, or where, but she loved it and did not want to leave. She wanted more.

After a couple of months of many laughs and good times with Richard and his friends, he asked her to fly to Las Vegas with him and his friend Ray on Ray's private jet. Ray was the founder and CEO for a chain of gas stations situated all over the West. She had met Ray before and agreed to go to Vegas for a weekend, but only under the condition she would have her own room, with no strings attached. He agreed and made arrangements for them. They stayed in Las Vegas and ended up having a good time hanging out with his friends and seeing a concert. He loved showing Kay off, as she was by far the youngest woman he had ever dated. Not only was she the youngest, but he could not believe how mature she was for her age. Little did he know that she had already lived several lives. Kay never shared her secrets with anyone, and she always knew how to pretend everything was alright, even in the midst of a disaster. With Richard, she was able to be more open about her past, but only her past relationships with men. She would come close to telling him about her father but never did. Like everyone else, Richard assumed Kay's father had died in a car accident.

Richard was falling in love with Kay. She loved spending time with him, and that was it for her. She loved having him as a friend. She had girlfriends, but most of them were married and hated that Kay hung around with Richard. They thought it was strange that she would go and hang out with him and his friends, due to his age, but Kay did not care. He was good for her self-esteem, which had been severely destroyed and damaged by her past. He wasn't a jealous person, and he took care of Kay. She felt she had a fresh start because of his friendship, like Lori all over again. She saw a bright future ahead. She was not sure what would come next, but it had to be good.

99

It was fall, and Richard had a business trip planned to go to Victoria, British Columbia, and then was going to take the clipper to Seattle. He loved Victoria Island and Seattle. He wanted Kay to meet him there, so he pulled out all the stops to persuade her. He booked her a room of her own and paid for her to leave Lauren with her parents for several nights and meet him there. Kay was reluctant but excited. She would be flying to Vancouver and then take a flight over to Victoria alone. It was a dream to be able to see new places and to do it first class was overwhelming. She loved the excitement of it all, but she also longed to be in love—not just jetting off to places just to see them. Still, in love or not, she could not resist the temptation to be able to travel and see new things she had longed to see since she was a child. She was seeing the world through another window, and it most certainly wasn't an old bus.

Kay enjoyed her trip to Victoria, and it was as beautiful as she had heard and hoped it would be. There were hanging potted plants overflowing with flowers on every light post, and the island felt magical. She really enjoyed taking the clipper to Seattle. It was her first time witnessing such plush green beauty surrounded by deep blue water, and she loved being on the Puget Sound. As the clipper pulled into Seattle, it took her breath away. It was a sunny, beautiful day in Seattle, and they were able to visit Pike's Market and walk around the city. They had a nice dinner before they flew back to Salt Lake City that same evening. Kay was in awe, and Richard knew it. He immediately asked her for a favor, which would lead to him spending more time with her.

He had a business trip planned in Florida and then immediately after that he needed to be in Monterey California. He asked if Kay she could meet him in San Jose to drive him from the San Jose airport to Monterey. He explained the drive was two hours long and he would be too exhausted to drive himself. Kay had no idea what he was talking about, as she had never been to the Bay Area and did not understand why he could not drive himself to Monterey. He was a smart man, and he knew exactly what he was doing. Still, she agreed to go, so he booked her a room in Monterey.

It was around nine p.m. when she touched down in San Jose and met up with Richard. While she was driving him to Monterey, it was so dark she could not see anything. She knew they were near the ocean, but could not see it.

After arriving at the hotel around eleven, he let her know he would be in meetings till five o'clock the next day. "Go walk around and enjoy the scenery," he said. They gave each other a hug good night and she went up to her room where she could hear the ocean waves.

The next morning, she drew the blinds open and was blown away! The view encouraged her to get ready in a hurry so she could check out the quaint little shops in Monterey. She spent most of the day sightseeing.

Richard had let her know they would be going to Carmel and having dinner that evening. When he finished, he called her room and asked her to meet him in the lobby. He took her along the seventeen-mile drive, allowing her to see some of the most beautiful ocean views in the world. He kept telling her he wanted to see the sunset at Carmel by the Sea. She had no idea what he was talking about. As far as she was concerned, the views she was already taking in were so beautiful that she wanted to pull over every half-mile or so to take pictures.

After they passed the famous Pebble Beach Golf club and Resort, she felt as if she had entered another world. They drove and came to a slope in the road where many cars were vying for a place to pull over and park. It was almost impossible to find a place to stop. When they did, Kay could see in the distance some cypress trees and in an opening there were people gathering. When she looked past the people, she saw large, powerful waves beating against the shore. They walked up to the white sand, which lead to a long, white, sandy slope with deep, dark, green jagged cypress trees topping the slope. It was beautiful! The white sand spanned down to gigantic waves that were crashing so hard against the shore that it shook the ground like heavy thunder. Kay was speechless as they started to walk down the hill. She found a place to sit to watch the sunset; for a moment, it was like she was at a fireworks show, only better—everyone was taking their seat to see the most beautiful show on Earth. Kay was completely mesmerized.

She could not hear or see Richard since she had just walked off on her own and found a place to bask in the beauty of that moment. It awoke her innermost romantic emotions, and in that moment, she desperately yearned to be in love. She knew he loved her and did not want to create an uncomfortable moment. It was the most beautiful, romantic place she had ever been to in her life, and she wanted to stay there forever. After the sun set, the sky began to turn different shades of purple and gray mixed with tints of orange. It was difficult for Kay to remove herself from where she had been sitting. As she mustered up the energy and willpower to move, she realized that the time she had been spending with Richard had not been spent falling in love with him, but rather with the scenery he kept handing to her on a silver platter.

On the flight home, he let her know that he had a trip planned to Maui, and he invited her to join him. She was becoming concerned about several things. One was leaving Lauren; she had left her so much over the past few months. Also, she knew with each trip she agreed to, he was falling more in love with her. The trip was set for late January, and it was late November, so she had time to plan and she wanted to go.

In December, Kay met a guy named Ian, who was introduced to her by a girl that worked in the same office building. Ian was instantly taken with Kay and asked her to go have a drink and play pool one evening after work. She was instantly attracted to him. He was tall, average build, with dark hair and a baby face.

She went out with him, and they had a great time. They immediately began sleeping together, but soon after that, she found out Ian had a girlfriend. Kay was furious and swore she would not see him again.

Richard found out about her and Ian and became jealous. He threatened if she saw Ian again, he would not take her to Maui. Still, Ian continued to pursue Kay and promised her he was leaving his girlfriend. She wanted to believe him because. After all, he was her age, and there was no denying she felt attracted to him. She hated the way Richard made her feel, guilty when they were just supposed to be friends. It was her fault and she knew it, but she wanted the best of both worlds. She could use Ian for what she wanted and needed and still be spoiled by a man that really loved her and wanted her. She did not love Ian and was just using him. It was complicated, and she knew something had to give. She just did not know what would happen next.

Richard found out she was seeing him again and followed through with his threat; he told her he was not going to take her to Maui. She was okay with it. After all, she did not love Richard, and this way, she would not have to leave Lauren again. She hoped things would settle down for her and be less complicated without Richard in her life. She had wished she could have it all—the love and the life Richard was offering her—but it just wasn't happening. She was twenty-seven, going on twenty-eight and needed to reevaluate her life.

* * *

Three days before Richard was ready to leave for Maui, he asked Kay to meet him for lunch. He told her he wished she was going with him and that he had made a mistake by telling her she couldn't come along. For some reason, a strange feeling came over her and she responded with, "It's not too late, you know."

103

He got excited and said, "Well, I will have to see if we can get you on the flight. Let me make some phone calls, and I will let you know. Be ready to go just in case."

She contacted Suzanne to make sure she could take care of Lauren. Within an hour, Richard called to tell her she would have to take another flight and meet him there because his flight was full. She was fine with that, so he booked her on another flight that arrived in Honolulu several hours after his. They planned to meet in Honolulu and fly to Maui together.

Kay felt a bit guilty about leaving Lauren again, but it she couldn't help but be excited. In three days, she would be in Maui. It was all so surreal.

She still had to beg her boss for the time off. She knew it really wasn't about the time off so much as the gossip in the office about how much traveling Kay was doing with Richard. Everyone knew who he was because his office was in the same building. He often sent Kay flowers, and his company was now one of their biggest clients. It was not advantageous for Kay, but she did not like the women she worked with anyway because they were catty and jealous.

Kay flew from Salt Lake to Los Angeles, where she had to change flights. When she got on the plane in Los Angeles, she took her seat in first class next to a man in his early forties. He instantly seemed interested in talking to her. He asked lots of questions about where she was from and if she had ever been to Hawaii. She was annoyed and just wanted to get the five-hour flight over with. He could sense she wanted to be left alone, so he did not bother trying to talk to her any longer.

About an hour into the flight, they ordered drinks, and the flight attendant accidentally spilled the man's drink on Kay. She had to go to the lavatory to clean up. When she returned, she decided to start a conversation with the man. His name was Matt, and he asked Kay what she did for a living. She let him know she was an employment recruiter in Salt Lake City. He then began volunteering information about himself, telling her he was a division manager for GTE and lived in Los Angeles. She responded with, "I love California, especially Monterey and the Carmel area."

He then told her he was looking for an outside sales representative in the Bay Area.

Kay jokingly asked, "Are you telling me this because you want me to help you recruit someone, or are you trying to hire me?"

He immediately responded and said, "I think you would be great for the job, and I know I just met you, but you are exactly the kind of person we have been looking for in northern California. You seem...personable, and, no, I am not just saying that to hit on you." He continued, "We need someone up in the Bay Area to help us with our existing customers and to make new sales. You would be able to go to Monterey and Carmel every weekend."

Kay said, "You're kidding right? I am on a plane going to Hawaii and getting a job offer to move to California? This is too good to be true!"

Matt responded, "Nope, not kidding. I am dead serious. Here is my card. Just call me when you get back from Hawaii, and we will set up a time to fly you in for an interview with one of my managers in San Jose."

Kay was in a state of shock. She had been drinking a few too many cocktails and couldn't stop the words, "You better not be fucking lying to me!" from flying out of her mouth.

Matt responded by laughing out loud and reassured Kay he wanted her for the job and he had enjoyed their visit. It was pretty much a done deal, but he still wanted her to fly to San Jose for a formal interview. She felt she was living a dream, and everything was in slow motion—one strange twist after the other.

As the plane descended into Honolulu, she couldn't figure out if she was more excited about seeing Hawaii or the whole new idea of moving to California. She was on cloud nine and could not wait to tell Richard.

Richard was waiting for Kay at the gate, and he could not wait to see her and share the flight from Hawaii to Maui together. Kay was immediately taken by the fresh air and feel of Hawaii. It was dusk, and she could barely grasp the beauty that surrounded her and what was happening. When she saw Richard, she gave him a great big hug, and he was so happy to see her. She was in such great spirits, and he hoped it was all because she would be spending time with him, but as soon as they walked out to board their flight and Kay started to tell Richard about everything that had just transpired, he was completely caught off guard. He seemed to get more and more bothered as Kay shared with him what she believed to be her miracle encounter with Matt on the other plane. She could not understand why his demeanor had changed from happy to a red scowl, but he exploded, "You naïve, gullible child! What in the fuck are you thinking, believing anything a stranger tells you? That man was trying to pick you up. Do you actually think he is interested in hiring you?"

Kay was so upset. She had thought Richard would be happy for her good fortune and amazing good luck. Instead, he was being a total asshole. She started to cry and snapped back at him, "You don't know what in the hell you are talking about! Maybe you think because you did not want to hire me and you just wanted to pick me up that everyone is that way! Well, Richard, that's bullshit! I have his business card, and I am to call him in two weeks to set up a time to fly to San Jose! I don't care if you believe me or not. He is not an asshole who is just trying to get in my pants, and he really wants me to work in the Bay Area!"

Richard knew he had gone too far because he had never seen her so upset. He just wanted to enjoy the trip, so he apologized and told her gently that she should not get her hopes up just in case nothing came of her so-called fortuitous flight.

She accepted his apology and let him know she was warned and would not be hurt if Matt ended up being a liar. "I'll be fine either way," she said, but secretly she knew she really would be hurt if Matt turned out to be playing her.

It was obviously a sore subject, so Richard suggested they avoid discussing it so they could have a good time in Maui, and that's exactly what they did. Kay was able to experience a helicopter ride and sailing on the ocean for the first time. It was gorgeous, and once again she wished she had someone she was in love with, to share the beautiful moments with. But deep down, she was falling in love with another scenic view and daydreaming about the possibility that she would be living and working in sunny California. She would be able to see the ocean whenever she wanted to if Matt kept his promise and hired her. She was twenty-seven years old, unsure of what would happen next. It seemed as though it had been years since Kay had woken to the nightmare of her father's suicide, and she hoped those terrible nighttime recollections would never haunt her again. Kay needed change, and she was hoping that memorable flight from Los Angeles to Hawaii would lead to a better future.

* * *

Kay decided it was best to keep the whole California opportunity under wraps from her family and friends until she was sure it was going to happen. Weeks passed, and Kay finally dialed Matt's number with butterflies in her stomach. She was so nervous and paranoid that he would not remember her or that he was lying. He answered her call and let her know it would be a couple of weeks before he could set up a time for her to meet him and the manager in San Jose. "I'll give you a call when it's a good time," he assured her.

For the following two weeks, she had her doubts about Matt's commitment. She tried bringing up the subject with Richard, but each time it was the same old

107

story: "I told you not to trust him. He was just a stranger trying to tell you what you wanted to hear. Let it go."

But Kay couldn't let it go. She kept her vow to never tell a soul (besides Richard) that she might be leaving for California—at least not until she had to.

A month passed, and Kay still had not heard from Matt. She was ready to give up hope, but she decided to call him once again. This time, he apologized for not getting back to her and let her know he wanted her to fly into San Jose the following week. Matt said he would have his secretary call with flight information and details, as she would be flying in early in the morning and flying out the same afternoon. She immediately called Richard to tell him about it, and he was speechless.

Kay called in sick that following Wednesday, and Richard drove her to the airport. He apologized as she was getting out of his car and told her he was sure they would make an offer. However, he did not think she would have the guts to actually make the move. He let her know he would be there to pick her up when she returned that evening.

Kay had never been so nervous in her entire life. This was the biggest thing that had ever happened to her. She was going to California on her own, without anyone knowing. Her dream of becoming an outside sales representative could be coming true. She searched and searched and finally found the perfect suit, along with a light pink blouse. She looked polished, professional, and felt beautiful she was ready to make her move.

It was a nerve-racking flight, but once Kay arrived in San Jose and met up with Matt, her nerves quieted down a bit. They took a rental car to a beautiful little town called Los Gatos, where she met his manager, Steve, for the formal interview. She was nervous to meet Steve, but once they all sat down together, she was fine.

The interview process entailed verbal questions and a written test, much more than Kay had anticipated. She figured she was just flying in to get the job offer, and she had no idea it would be so intense. She survived the three hours of testing and questioning, and then they all had lunch together before Matt took her back to the airport. She was finally able to breathe a sigh of relief. She knew she had done the best she could. Now, it was just a waiting game since they told her it would be weeks before she heard anything from them.

A month passed, and once again and Kay was disappointed, assuming she did not get the job. Anytime she brought the subject up to Richard, he let her know there was a distinct possibility they had found someone else to fill the position. He was sure since they had not contacted her after four weeks, they did not want to hire her after all, and secretly, he was relieved.

Several more weeks passed, and after a bad day with work, she decided she had nothing to lose by contacting Steve to get some closure. She had a bad feeling as she sat in her office and made the call. When Steve got on the phone and realized it was her, he began apologizing and explained that he thought Matt had already called to let her know they would be making an offer. That was her first little taste of corporate America: miscommunication and no follow-through. She felt butterflies with heat rising up to her head, and could feel her face turn bright red. She was absolutely happy! He told her they were looking at offering her thirty five thousand a year, plus a car. She was taken aback because Matt had told her the job paid more than that. She let Steve know she thought the salary was around fifty thousand, and Steve explained that pay was commensurate with experience, and since she had no experience in outside sales, she would have to start out low and work her way up. Evidently, Steve was trying to do something else common in corporate America: lowball her and wait for a counteroffer. But when he heard the disappointment in her voice, he let her know they would be paying for her to relocate, as well as a five thousand dollar signing bonus.

She asked him to give her twenty-four hours to think about it.

She immediately called Richard, who thought Kay was over the California dream. He was planning his next adventure in hopes he could allure Kay into going with him once again. He was sitting in his office when he received the call.

"Guess what," she said. "They made me an offer!"

There was silence on the other end of the phone.

"Did you hear me?"

Richard was in complete shock, for he truly believed Kay would never hear from Matt's company again. He felt a dagger move through his chest as he barely could say words, "You're kidding me!"

She then told him that they would be paying for her move, as well as giving her a five thousand dollar signing bonus. They needed her to start right away, and she needed to be in Los Angeles for training in one week. Richard was dumbfounded and asked her what she was going to do, to which she responded, "Well, of course I am taking the job."

His heart sank, and he asked her to meet him in the lobby. As she walked out of the office past all the women who hated her, she was laughing inside. She met Richard downstairs, and he picked her up in his arms and hugged her tightly, fighting back tears. He asked her if she was sure she wanted to leave, and Kay looked him in the eyes and said, "Absolutely! I told you on the flight going to Maui that I would move if they offered me the job, and I meant it." He couldn't believe it was all happening so quickly.

Kay spent the next few days looking on the Internet—a brand new concept in the late 1998—to find an apartment. She broke the news to everyone while preparing for the move. The moving people came to her apartment and wrapped each dish and her belongings ever so carefully. They loaded it all into a moving truck. It was all quite ironic, considering her experience as a child and the old bus, but that was all in the past.

Lauren was very upset and cried when she heard the news. She did not want to go. She clung to her grandparents just like Kay had when she was ten years old and they had to board the old musty bus to leave Ohio. She knew Lauren would be alright, but it was going to take time. This was a good exciting move, one that would open doors in hers and Lauren's lives. She could not pass up this opportunity, and she felt it was destined. She had been nothing but trailer trash, traveling as a poser with a wealthy man. She wanted so badly to travel and live a good life on her own terms without owing anyone anything. She wanted to change her surroundings and meet new people. That is exactly what Kay needed, and Matt was giving her that chance.

Living in California, she would get to see and do so many things most of her friends and family could only dream of. She believed she was giving her daughter a better life in every way.

Suzanne was upset and angry with Kay for keeping everyone in the dark about the possible job and move. She and Kay fought a lot during that time, and Kay finally told her mother that she was under enough stress and that if she was going to keep piling on the guilt, she would not talk to her at all. After that threat, Suzanne started to calm down, apologized, and began reluctantly supporting Kay's decision. It helped ease her pain knowing she would keep Lauren until Kay got settled.

Jesse's grandmother, on the other hand, was livid! She hated Kay and her plan to move, but she had no legal say in what Kay did with Lauren. Luckily for Kay, Jesse had written his paternal privileges off years earlier.

For the first time, Lauren finally was able to understand why they moved to California, and it made her feel better about the painful memories she had about the move. She could no longer hold a grudge against her mother for that particular move, for now she knew that move was a once-in–a-lifetime opportunity that Kay could not turn down. I wouldn't have turned it down either, Lauren realized. Knowing her mother's dreams and motives, especially after her painful past, was like a healing balm, soothing some of the pain she had experienced when she left her family in Utah at age six. Questions were being answered for Lauren—questions she'd never been brave enough to ask—and she had to read on to find the answers.

11

It was a hot day in July when Kay loaded the last of her belongings into her car. She kissed Lauren goodbye and promised her she would see her in three weeks. She had to leave early for California so she could go through training for her new job and get their apartment put together before Lauren came to join her there. She knew it was going to be a difficult and huge transition for Lauren, for Kay herself had been through it when she was young. But she also knew Lauren would be okay in time, and for now she was safe with her grandparents.

Kay was filled with excitement as she waved goodbye and headed out across the desert alone. She actually looked forward to the long drive. She had the music blaring and was in a zone of pure happiness and relief. Her painful past was becoming more and more distant, and with each mile marker, she was putting it behind her. When she reached the Utah-Nevada border, she could not help but cry she was so happy. As she looked out at the vast desert, a feeling of complete freedom overwhelmed Kay. She was no longer was tied to a desk, an assembly line, or a bad relationship. She had all the time in the world to daydream of her new life. It was the first time as an adult that Kay had ever felt a real sense of peace, it was just like the one she felt as a small child laying in her yard and watching the planes overhead.

She had always enjoyed driving and the freedom it allowed, but this drive was special. Even though she was moving to a place where she did not know anyone, she had a feeling of calmness, a sense that finally, nobody and nothing could hurt her. She felt safer in the middle of nowhere than when she was surrounded by people.

The adrenaline from the excitement and the closure of the past were both rushing through her mind as she felt the comfort and security in her vehicle. She felt her spirit rising as she traversed the open road.

She was getting the hell out of Utah, away from all the pain and difficulty she had as a result of being surrounded by Mormons, especially as an adolescent.

She always believed that the religion had taken from her a chance at a normal life. Sean had been her first and only love. Over the years she thought about him. She knew that he had married shortly after seeing Kay in the hospital when Lauren was born. She heard that he and his wife had several children and were living in an old farm house on his father's land. *What if I had been Mormon? What if Sean hadn't been, would I be there with him now?* These bitter sweet thoughts crossed Kay's mind often especially during her travels with Richard.

Although her life had not been anywhere close to ideal; she knew the many twists of fate had helped her to see the world in a way she could never have imagined.

The past was the past, and in her young, naïve mind, Kay believed life could not possibly shell out anything worse than what she'd already been through. This was a new beginning, a chance to enjoy and explore an area she had always assumed she would only dream of. It was all because of Richard! Besides living near the ocean and going into San Francisco whenever she felt like it, meeting new people—maybe a successful man—maybe finding love again, anything seemed possible.

She couldn't wait to bond with Lauren while taking advantage to see everything she could. She was determined to make sure Lauren was comfortable and loved living there.

* * *

Three weeks passed by quickly, and Kay was enjoying her new world. She truly believed she had finally found her home and was already making the best of the luck she had. She wanted nothing more than to forget her horrible past. The only hurdle she had left was to be sure her seven-year-old loved the place as much as she did.

She knew Lauren was going to be upset about the move, and it would be hard for her, but she was not prepared for the moment she went to pick her daughter up at the airport. Lauren had been escorted by a flight attendant to her mother. She ran to her mother in tears and told her she wanted to go back to Utah; she did not want to leave her grandparents and family. Kay tried to reassure her it was all for the best and that one day she would thank her for moving her away from Utah. She told Lauren she was going to get to experience things and live a life that any little girl would be lucky to live. Kay could not understand why her baby was not excited to go and see the big city, the ocean, or the amazing famous bridges. Nevertheless, all Lauren could talk about and do for months on end was cry for the family they'd left behind.

* * *

After several months of living in and enjoying the Bay Area, Kay began to feel lonely. Her expectations of easily meeting people were shattered. She watched thousands of people each day, hustling and bustling here and there. She watched millions of cars jamming the freeways. She felt as if she were on an island all alone, watching the world pass her by. The gorgeous views and seascapes and amazing places in the city just weren't cutting it. She needed companionship.

Fortunately, after some time, Lauren began to adjust, and things were good with work. The only thing missing were friends, a partner, an adult to spend time with.

Richard had come to visit and they had a wonderful evening catching up while having dinner in San Francisco. She let him know that she was worried she may never meet anyone and the move to California may have been a huge mistake. He let her know she had done the right thing in leaving Utah and that he was proud of her. He comforted her and reassured her she would eventually meet new people, she just needed to be patient. She was grateful for his support and knew he loved her; it was comforting knowing he was in her life and they would always be good friends.

* * *

Several weeks after Richard had come to visit Kay she received a call from her mother Suzanne. She had never heard her mother's voice stutter in the way it did as she relayed the news that Richard had been killed.

He and Ray were flying to from Salt Lake City to Portland Oregon when Ray's jet crashed somewhere in Idaho. Suzanne had heard about it on the local news and called Kay right away. Kay was crushed and devastated.

If it hadn't been for meeting Richard she would have never been able to see the world through in different light. She would have never had built up the self -esteem and confidence to move to California and would have never had the opportunity to do so if it hadn't been for him. He had meant so much to her and had changed her life in a positive way, a way that no other person had. He had been unexpected surprise in her life. Richard had been the only person in her life that told her how beautiful she was. He had breathed life into her and made her feel worthy of being loved, now he was gone. She mourned his death for weeks. She would miss him forever. Kay felt lonelier than ever knowing Richard was gone, knowing she couldn't pick up the phone and call him to tell him what was happening in her life. It was a gigantic loss for her. She had lost another best friend.

Laurens hands shook as she read her mother's memories of that time. Tears filled her eyes as she remembered how completely distraught her mother became when hearing the news of Richards death. She remembered trying to comfort her mother by hugging her as she cried. She felt so bad for her mom and knew that Richard had meant so much to her.

She looked out the window and stared at the flashing light on the wing of the plane, she couldn't help but realize now what a huge part Richard had played in changing her own life.

12

Kay's job was a remote position, and she was telecommuting with an office out of Los Angeles and would drive there once in a while. She had fun with co-workers while in Los Angeles but did not have any co-workers in the area where she was living. The loneliness was becoming difficult.

It was right around the holidays, and she had gone back to Utah to visit her parents for Thanksgiving, her favorite holiday. Lauren didn't want to leave her family to go back to California. Kay knew what Lauren was feeling; she had experienced the same feeling as a child. She hoped Richard had been right about Kay meeting new people and she had done the right thing in leaving Utah.

* * *

She spent many hours on the phone talking with old friends, including her friend Lori, who was still in Maryland.

Lori had left Ben after only a year of marriage for another man. Ben and Lori never really connected on an intellectual level, as he had a dry sense of humor and wanted to stay home all time playing videogames and Lori liked to be out and about. When it came to that, they were like oil and water, and they argued all the time. Lori had an affair with their neighbor, a married man named Eddie. He and his wife were having difficulties also, and the two ended up falling in love as they were commiserating with each other. Each left their marriages in order to be together.

Ben was understandably angry and devastated when Lori told him she was leaving him, so he moved back to Utah to be near his family and get his bearings. He had even tried to get in touch with and hang out with Kay, but Kay never felt comfortable befriending her friend's ex. Even though she did like his personality and he could make her laugh, she did not feel comfortable hanging around him after he and Lori split up. Something about it just didn't feel right.

On one of her phone calls to Lori, Kay started to cry and told Lori how lonely she was becoming living in the Bay Area. She told Lori she wished she knew someone she could hang out with. Lori then paused for a long time, and Kay asked, "Are you there?"

Lori responded, "Okay, I wasn't going to tell you this, but Ben is living in the Bay Area now."

Kay said, "Ben? Ben who?"

Lori responded, "You know. My ex-husband Ben!"

"Oh, really? What is he doing here, and where exactly does he live?"

"San Jose, and I don't care if you contact him. I understand that you're alone there, and he may know some people for you to hang out with. After all, he is a scientist and seems to be doing well."

Kay asked her how she knew where Ben was all these years. She told her they had to work out old financial tax issues with the home they had bought together. She had just spoken to him just thirty days prior. She then explained, "I would have...well, I woulda told you sooner, but for a moment it bothered me that you guys are both living in the Bay Area at the same time. I don't know why, because I am so in love and happy with Eddie that it shouldn't matter. Anyway, call Ben. I am sure you guys will hook up, and that is okay with me. Even if you have to use him for—you know—I will understand."

Kay screamed, "Oh, hell, Lori! What? I am just excited to think that maybe I can meet people through Ben, and we can be friends. It would be too weird to hook up with him, and I would feel guilty."

Lori let Kay know it did not matter and gave her Ben's phone number. She told Kay to let her know if they ended up getting together. She told her she loved her and that they would keep in touch.

Kay could not help being excited, but she still felt weird about the whole situation of contacting Ben. He had always seemed to like Kay, and Kay knew he could offer a built-in connection to some successful men. After all, Ben was a scientist in Silicon Valley. Ben had always loved Kay's wit and sarcasm. She was always laughing about something and had a contagious laugh. Kay had programmed herself to take even the worst circumstance and poke fun, even if it was in the middle of crying; she could literally start laughing through her tears. No matter how much pain she was in, she would crack a sarcastic line and have everyone rolling. Ben had the same personality, so when Ben received Kay's message, he called her right back.

He sounded so excited to hear she lived in Pleasanton, which was approximately forty miles from San Jose. Ben, Kay, and Kelsey ended up having dinner. Ben asked Kay if she could come to San Jose the next night for karaoke with all of his friends from work. Kay was excited to finally get out of the house and agreed. She got a sitter for Lauren and headed down to San Jose in the hopes of meeting lots of eligible men. Little did Kay know that all of Ben's friends were women!

Ben had a fan club, and it seemed as if he was the only single White male within a one hundred mile radius. It was the dot.com era, and more and more people were moving into the Bay Area as time marched toward the dot.com era. There may have been more men in Silicon Valley at that time than anywhere else in the world. However, all of them seemed to be Indian or Asian. Kay was not racist, but she was and had always been attracted to White men.

Ben was a Jack Mormon who claimed that he did not believe in any religion, but if he had to choose, he would say Mormon. He was extremely charming. He loved singing Sinatra songs and was so good at it that he always got standing ovations for his impressions of Old Blue Eyes.

Kay was amazed and intrigued with Ben's world, and she was happy to finally be enjoying herself in California, even though she could feel the heat of jealousy burning through her back as she and Ben talked and hung out that evening.

At one point, Ben got up to sing and said, "This one is for Kay."

All the women who had crushes on Ben were annoyed and gave her dirty looks.

Kay wanted to leave early because she had a long drive home, but Ben kept asking her to wait. Andrea, who had a mad crush on Ben, offered to take Kay to her car, but her plan to get Kay out of the picture backfired because Ben agreed and told Andrea to take both of them to Kay's car, which was parked at Ben's apartment.

After Andrea reluctantly dropped them off, Ben invited Kay in for a nightcap. They sat on his couch and talked till two in the morning before Kay remembered she had a forty-mile drive home and that she must get on the road. Ben insisted she stay at his place and said she could sleep on the sofa. Kay decided that would be a good idea. After getting comfortable on Ben's sofa with a blanket and pillow, she started to doze off.

Ben quietly whispered, "Kay, you know, you could sleep in here in my bed. It might be much more comfortable."

Because she had had a touch too much to drink at the karaoke bar and because it had been months since Kay had had sex, the offer was appealing. The thought of just being held by a man, even for one evening, was more important than loyalty to an old friend. So, Kay took Ben up on his offer and crawled into bed with him.

The next day, she woke up in Ben's bed and felt horrible. *What have I done? What about Lori? She said it was okay, but did she really mean it?* Kay was torn. Finally, she was having fun for the first time in a long time, but in the process, she felt like the worst friend in the world.

Ben and Kay spent every night together after that, usually at her apartment in Pleasanton. Ben commuted every night to be with her and Lauren. He adored Lauren, and Kay felt safe with Ben. Even though she knew it was going to compromise her relationship with Lori, she needed him. Kay was not in love with Ben, but he offered her something she desperate needed to combat her big-city loneliness: companionship. It wasn't but maybe thirty days when Ben had made the decision to give up his apartment in San Jose and to move in with Kay and Lauren.

Things were moving so quickly. Kay woke up with a whole new set of nightmares, terrified of how Lori would react when she found out she was waking up next to Ben because she was living together. Kay knew she was risking her longtime friendship, even though she was not in love with Ben, but the beautiful California sunsets were simply not enough; she needed and craved companionship in her new world. Kay was doing her best to rationalize her behavior, and she avoided calling Lori. The silence between them was nothing new. There had been times in their lives when they would not talk for months because they lived across the country from each other. Each had their own lives, and they were busy taking care of others.

Finally, three months later, the day came when Kay received the call from Lori. The first words out of Lori's mouth were, "So, did you and Ben hook up? I want to know. I told you it was okay, and I understand you were lonely. If he can make you feel better, then good for you! Just please tell me."

Kay was silent.

Lori continued, "It's okay, Kay. You can tell me, and I won't be mad. I am in love with Eddie, and Ben is just part of my past. Seriously, just be honest with me. I will be fine with it either way. I just...I just need to know."

Kay was not worried about telling Lori she had hooked up with Ben, but him moving in with her was a different story. Kay finally responded with part of the truth, "Yes, I hooked up with Eddie."

Lori roared "I knew it! Don't worry. It's okay, and I'm not mad about it. I had a feeling that would happen, I love you, Kay. You're my friend, and nothing is ever going to change that,"

Kay said, "Well, there is more."

Lori sounded surprised. "Huh? What?"

Kay took a deep breath and let the words she had been dreading fall from her tongue. "We are living together, Ben and me."

There was a long silence on the other end of the phone, but then Kay asked if Lori was still there, and she responded with a choked-up voice, "Yes."

Kay started crying and explained to Lori that she was sorry and that it all just happened. Lori was shocked but told Kay she understood. She told Kay she was worried that Ben might come between her and Kay's relationship. Lori knew Ben hated her and believed he might be trying to hurt her by being with Kay. They spent hours on the phone reassuring each other that nothing—Ben or otherwise—would ruin their friendship.

* * *

Ben was a computer geek, but he also liked to go golfing now and then. He enjoyed hitting balls at the driving range. Lauren loved Ben, and they just clicked. Between videogames, golf, and the banter, Lauren was having fun.

One Saturday, Ben told Kay he was going to the golf course to hit some balls, and Lauren asked if she could tag along. They returned several hours later, and Ben seemed excited. Ben was so caught off guard by Lauren's natural ability to hit the golf ball that he decided to buy her, her very own club—one that was her size—so she could go to the driving range with him whenever he went, which was often. Lauren seemed quite excited about golf. Kay had seen her excited about soccer, softball, and basketball, so she wasn't at all surprised when her child of seven years old had a new obsession. So, when Ben and Lauren returned with their exciting story of how well Lauren hit the ball, Kay brushed it off.

Kay had no experience with golf herself, and what happened at the golf course did not interest her. She thought it was a boring sport that took way too long to play. She didn't understand it and considered it a waste of time. She had only heard of words like "backswing," "par," and "country club" and had never given them much thought.

She did enjoy the view from Pebble Beach when they drove there on weekends, but she hated stopping anywhere near the country club because she felt so out of place. In her head, she was still that little White trash girl and felt she did not fit in. Even though she traveled with Richard and was able to visit the land of the rich, she knew it was not a world she had earned herself. Because she was only riding his coattails and had not earned her ticket on her own, she felt it wasn't right to be there. She could only to drive by and dream. She thought of golf as a pretentious, expensive sport, and she did not have the money to really afford to live in the Bay Area; she was only there like a tourist, wanting to experience and see it without ever really belonging to it. She knew there was no way in hell she would be able to afford to support Lauren if golf and the wealthy golf culture did become her new obsession.

Nevertheless, Ben continued to take Lauren with him to the driving range and continued to come home with story after story of how even the men would stop to watch

Lauren drive the ball, purely amazed at her natural swing. Kay only thought, *so? How hard can it possibly be to hit a little white ball?* Kay did not understand how well Lauren played; only that she was supposedly good at it.

Lauren loved Ben and felt close to him, and they spent hours playing video games and competing at just about anything they could. But Kay was growing a bit envious of the time they spent together. She was lonely and wanted someone to get out and experience the Bay Area with her. When they wouldn't go, she decided to venture out on her own.

Kay found her peace by driving over to the coast on the weekends. She learned to enjoy going by herself, when she didn't have to listen to Lauren and Ben complain that they would rather be on a golf course or playing videogames. Ben was usually tired of commuting all week, and the last thing he wanted to do was get in the car and drive forty miles just to look at the ocean.

* * *

Because of Richard Kay had become obsessed with wanted to see the beauty of world, though, and out of necessity, she was getting used to seeing it all alone. She enjoyed the scenery and freedom so much that she didn't care if others did not understand or take part in her adventures. She would just drive and enjoy her daydreams along the way. She sometimes would take her bike and ride it over the Golden Gate Bridge. She spent almost every single weekend somewhere different. She went to Carmel, Monterey, and Half Moon Bay to watch the sunset by herself. She fully appreciated the sites and sound of the ocean. She would lie on the beach not to sunbathe, but just to sit and look out over the vast span of never-ending water. To Kay, it was the edge of the world. She was a romantic unaware, and as her love affair with beautiful views was growing. Kay only wished she had someone to share the beauty with, someone who could understand her

125

appreciation for all the places she visited. She wanted real love but never wanted to be hurt again.

Meanwhile, Lauren's love for golf was intensifying, and her homesickness for Utah and her family there was getting better with each visit to the golf course with Ben.

Lauren stopped reading and started to reminisce. She remembered how much she enjoyed spending time with Ben. It was one of the best times of her life. She also remembered mother wanted nothing more than to live next to the ocean someday. She was gone almost every weekend and would come home with stories of how gorgeous the views were and how they had missed out, but neither of them cared, they were having too much fun playing video games.

13

Things for Kay were going well. She had been promoted at work and was moved into a new division within GTE, which meant she got a new office in San Ramon. She loved her new office and the people that worked there. One of those people was Ken, the typical guy at work that every woman wanted and anyone could have for at least one night. Kay knew his history and was not one to pursue known playboys. She had become so confident over the past several years that she had learned to say exactly what was on her mind, and Ken loved that about her. He thought Kay was beautiful and funny, two qualities that were not easy to find. He also knew she was living with a man because he sometimes overheard Kay talking about her relationship to one of her co-workers. He always seemed to find a way to be in the vicinity of where Kay's office was located. She knew he was attracted to her because he was always coming up with ways to tease her and play pranks on her. Kay was starting to realize he made her blush, and she was finding it more difficult each day to hide her infatuation with him.

She dreaded going home from work because she knew she and Ben were headed nowhere. They were basically just roommates, saving money by sharing expenses. It was not easy to find an apartment in Silicon Valley during the dot.com boom without being on a waiting list, and in order to be put on the waiting list, a person needed to have at least four thousand dollars up front. It was a stressful time, and Kay and Ben broke into fights constantly. She often told Ben he needed to find another place to live, but he could not find anything.

As her infatuation for Ken grew into passion, she could not hold back any longer. Kay and Ken's relationship was becoming more and more personal. Ken had a son, about the same age as Lauren, so they sometimes met up after work and took the kids to the park. On Halloween, they even took them trick-or-treating.

Ben had a feeling Kay was into someone else often accused her of it. The truth was that Kay and Ben had discussed him finding his own place for months before she had even met Ken. Once things started to heat up with Ken, Kay started to push Ben even harder to move out. The real problem was that Lauren loved Ben. With him gone, Lauren would have no one to help her with her golf aspirations, as Kay certainly wasn't the kind to take to the green. Kay knew it was going to be difficult for Lauren to see Ben go since she was so attached to him.

Kay needed and longed to feel loved and have somebody with similar interests in her life. However, what she was really feeling with Ken was passion. Her lust for him outweighed the fact he was just another loser, and once again she was blinded with a desperate need to connect with someone who would properly love her back.

Ben finally found a place back in San Jose. Of course he was hurt over Kay wanting to be with someone else, as well as not being able to spend time with Lauren. But the benefit was he no longer had to spend two hours commuting back and forth to work. He was relieved in a way, and he did not go without finding women to spend his time with; they were lined up around the block to date Ben.

Kay was falling in love and falling fast. Ken seemed to be completely obsessed with Kay's outgoing and happy demeanor. She had a glow about her, something he lacked. She found him to be sexy, someone she was passionate with. Ken's son Ryan he both liked to play videogames, so Lauren at least had someone around to ease the loss of her buddy Ben. While she enjoyed hanging out with Ryan, Lauren did not like Ken. She felt he was dark and didn't have a good personality like Ben. She didn't feel comfortable around him, but she knew her mother loved him.

Kay and Ken began spending a lot of time together, and they had discussed a shared future. After a year of spending as much time as humanly possible with one another, they started to discuss moving in together. Kay had no idea what he had in store for her and how that decision would affect hers and her daughter's lives.

One night while they were at a Giants game, during the seventh inning stretch, Ken actually got down on one knee and proposed to Kay. She was dumbfounded and in shock, and when she realized everyone was watching on the jumbo screen, she was overwhelmed. She wrapped her arms around Ken, and they kissed. The crowd roared and clapped with excitement, knowing they were witnessing a special moment. He gave her a beautiful ring. It was nothing fancy, but Kay did not care. She was in love and could not wait to start picking out wedding gowns.

Lauren, on the other hand, was becoming increasingly annoyed with her new future little brother. She thought he was a brat, especially since he cried every time he lost any game they were playing. She was not happy about the fact her mother was marrying Ken.

They set a wedding date for August, leaving Kay three months to plan the wedding. She wanted everything to be perfect for her, as it was her first—and hopefully her last—marriage. Her life was finally the way she wanted it to be, and for the first time, she felt all her dreams were coming true. The wedding was to be held in Lake Tahoe. It was so beautiful there, and it was a great place for her family from Utah and his from Oregon to meet. Suzanne and Mark even planned to meet up with Kay on her wedding day.

Lauren always spent several summer months in Utah, and while she was there, she played golf with her grandfather. He would often comment about Lauren's natural swing. Even though Kay couldn't have cared less about chasing a little white ball around eighteen holes with a club, as a mother she was intrigued to hear from more than one person that Lauren had a natural talent.

Once, in the middle of July, after Lauren had been in Utah for several weeks, Kay started to notice changes in Ken, or so she thought. She assumed maybe she just wasn't seeing him for who he really was until cracks in their relationship started to appear. She noticed some of the same characteristics that his son Ryan exhibited, like being a sore loser. Still, she overlooked his flaws, his moodiness, and the fact that he could be cruel at times. He even made rude comments about Kay's weight. She had always been thin, so she did not seem to notice that she had gone from a size two to a size four. She had finally conquered her feelings of inadequacy and of being self-conscious years ago while being around both Richard and Ben since both men loved her appearance and complimented her all the time.

Now, she began noticing that her self-esteem that had taken her years to build was being eroded little by little by Ken. In reality, he wanted her to feel inferior to him. She was always upbeat, as that was her nature in spite of everything, and he started to do whatever he could to upset her or make her cry. Kay remained in denial and did not want to believe that her future husband was a real asshole.

Things became even worse between them when Kay got yet another promotion. Her star was shining brightly in her career. She had always been a hard worker, and it was starting to pay off. Ken worked for GTE, in building maintenance, running the engineering department for the buildings GTE owned in San Ramon. While he hated his job, Kay loved hers. She hated to see him unhappy because she loved him so much, and she thought a change in careers would make him feel better.

Her subconscious was telling her to run, but she could not let go. She continued making plans for the wedding and sent out the invitations. Several days after the invitations were in the mail, Ken called her at work. He sounded distraught, and Kay asked him what was wrong.

131

He answered in a shaky, unstable voice, "I can't marry you. I don't love you. I am in love with someone else."

Kay dropped the phone and stared at her computer screen in shock. Not knowing what else to do, she got up and ran into the restroom. She was at work and did not know how to get out of the office building without anyone seeing her. She knew she had to get to her car, but she could barely walk due to the tremendous blow she had been dealt with that cowardly phone call. The son of a bitch did not even have the decency to tell her face to face, and to make matters worse, he broke the news to her while she was at work. She was mortified and knew he wanted to hurt her in a way so profound that would piss her off so she would just walk away without him having to see the hurt on her face. He was not only hurting her personally, but he was sabotaging her at work by making her an emotional wreck. It was the worst timing possible. All she knew was that she needed to get home as quickly as possible.

Peggy, one of Kay's co-workers, had seen Kay run into the restroom and was trying to console her. She helped her make it to her car and realized she needed to drive her home. Peggy knew Kay very well, and she also knew Ben. She called him to tell him what had happened, and Ben drove to Pleasanton to stay with Kay. He spent the night hugging her and consoling her as best he could, but she was completely out of it. He decided to take Kay to stay at his apartment in San Jose so he could keep an eye on her until she was able to process what had happened.

Ben still loved Kay as a friend. After all, they had known each other since they were eighteen. He adored Lauren and would do anything for her, including helping her mother through a horrific heartbreak. He got in touch with Suzanne and let her know what was happening and told her she may want to fly in to be with Kay during the trying time. Ben was pissed off about what Ken had done and wanted to kick his ass. He had never seen Kay so upset, and he was beside himself watching her rock in a corner, sobbing uncontrollably. She could not stop crying, but he knew there was nothing he could do for her except hope she would eventually run out of tears. She had chosen to be with Ken over him almost a year earlier, and it hurt him, but he was still trying to be there for her.

Kay cried so hard that her eyeballs felt as if they were coming out of the sockets. She was devastated, embarrassed and felt ruined. She could not believe what had happened, and Ken's cruel words on the phone kept playing over and over again in her head. She wanted to see Ken because it did not seem real. *Somehow...maybe he did not know what he was saying.*

Once Ben knew Suzanne would be arriving in several days to take care of Kay, and after her reassuring him she would be fine, Ben finally took her home. She was past the point of sadness and had reached the pissed-off phase. She wanted to see Ken; she needed to understand why. She had not looked in the mirror for two days, and when she did she did not recognize herself. Her face looked like a punching bag. Her eyes were red and puffy, almost swollen shut.

Seeing herself like that put her over the edge. She became enraged and decided to drag her tired and limp body to her car. Once she was inside the car, with the engine running, she drove like a bat out of hell to Ken's apartment and waited patiently for him to come home. She made sure to park her car so he would not see it. When he pulled up into his parking spot, she realized he had another woman in his car. As they both started to get out of his vehicle, Kay got out of her car and ran up behind him. She jumped on his back and started beating the shit out of him. She was raging and screaming, throwing punches and slapping him as much as she possibly could before he grabbed her arms to make her stop. She spit in his face and kicked him in the balls before screaming "You fucking loser! You did me a favor by getting the hell out of my life!"

The other woman looked at Kay like she was crazy.

Kay looked at her and said, "I feel sorry for you. He is a piece of shit, and he is all yours!" As Kay walked away, she yelled out, "You will be paying for all the wedding expenses, you son of a bitch!"

The other woman looked at Ken, confused, and yelled, "Wedding expenses? What wedding?"

Kay let out a laugh as she opened her car door to leave. The moment was so intense she could not believe it actually happened. She just wanted to wake up, but it was no dream. She turned on her car and peeled out of the parking lot. Incoherent, she drove to the nearest grocery store, where she bought three bottles of wine and two packs of cigarettes. She went home and guzzled wine and smoked until she passed out.

The next day, she woke to the nightmare she had hoped would never return. She always wanted to be able to run out of her father's house in time, in order to not witness the piercing sound of the gunshot and his blood splattered everywhere, but that was never how the dream—or the reality—turned out.

Lauren thought back to that time and she hated Ken and remembered how happy she was when the relationship ended.

Wow, it is amazing how one person can cause such a huge ripple effect, she thought to herself as she got up from her seat to use the lavatory, she then asked the Flight Attendant for another drink before settling back into her space again and continued to read.

14

Kay had been leveled by Ken. She felt as if the pain exceeded that of her first love with Sean, and it wasn't just because she was in the midst of planning their wedding when he broke it off. She was now thirty-one years old and felt as if her options and dreams were gone out the window and that she would never love like that again. Her heart was completely closed for business, and she had sacrificed her youth to nothing but heartache and pain.

Ken leaving her for another woman completely ruined any self-confidence she had left. Everything she had finally started to love and appreciate about herself was flushed down the toilet. She began throwing up every day from being sick with upset and unable to hold her food.

When Suzanne arrived, she could not believe what she saw. Her daughter looked like she had been in a fight. She was outraged and wanted to kill Ken herself. She did her best to console Kay, but she was only able to stay with her a few short days before she had to return back to work in Utah.

After her mother left to head back to the land of the Mormons, Kay lay on the floor and sobbed for days. Her weight plummeted from one hundred and twenty pounds to one hundred in a matter of weeks. One evening she sat and threw every dish she owned against a wall, it was her way of taking out her anger.

She had given up on the hope she had for California being a fresh start. Her past life was flashing before her eyes, and she could not tell anyone. She had to keep hiding her pain: her past life with an abusive father, an abusive relationship with a drug addict, and the pain of watching a murder-suicide. She could hardly function.

Fortunately, she was in outside sales and had the flexibility to work from home. She only had to attend a few excruciating appointments per week, and when she did, she managed to would put on a façade that everything was great. Once she left the meetings, she would get in her car, pull over to the side of the road, and cry. She missed Richard more than ever. He would have never allowed her to get so wrapped up in Ken, he wanted so much better for her.

Kay should have known better, but she wasn't always rational. The daydreaming and risk taking often felt more important than reality. In Kay's mind, the best feeling and time of her life was when she moved to California. So now, not being in her right mind, she thought of moving again to make everything all better, hoping to once again forget all the pain. She knew it had worked before, and there was no better time to try it again. She could barely go to work out of pure embarrassment, and the thought of running into Ken was worse than the fear she had in high school of running into Justin; Ken had pissed on her in a much more severe and humiliating manner.

* * *

While wanting to make changes, she was contacted by an employment recruiter who asked if she would be interested in going to work for more money at another telecommunications company, she immediately agreed to an interview. While in the interview, she mentioned that she wasn't sure she wanted to stay in the Bay Area. She said she would be open to working in another city, preferably Seattle. They loved Kay and told her they would set up an interview for her in Kirkland, just outside Seattle. Kay let out a sigh of relief knowing it might be her chance to escape her pain and have a fresh start.

She had a friend named Ann, and they would go to movies or have lunch once a week. Ann and her husband had moved to Seattle months earlier, so in late July, while Lauren was still visiting Utah, Kay decided to fly to Seattle and look around and spend some time with Ann before her interview. She had fallen in love with the city when she'd first laid eyes on it years earlier on a trip with Richard, so she was excited to go back again.

Kay drove from the SeaTac airport to downtown Seattle. It was so beautiful—even more gorgeous than she remembered. In some ways, she thought it was even more wonderful than San Francisco. She could not believe the deep blue water that spanned out to the islands and the city, and she knew right away she wanted to look for an apartment. She hoped it was a place where she could start over again. She had let Ken corrupt a place that she loved with all her heart, and she was no longer capable of looking at it the same way again. Ken had tarnished California for her, and it was time to move on.

The interview ended was not so much an interview as a question: "When can you start?" That gave her a bit of hope again, a spark that maybe things were going to turn around. It did not take her more than a day to find the apartment she wanted. It was located in Kirkland and had a view of Lake Washington. She could see Seattle in the distance, and it was perfect. She agreed to start the new job within the next three weeks.

On the flight back to Oakland, she thought about how difficult it would be to tell Lauren the news that they were moving again, and she was right. When Lauren heard they were moving again, she started crying. She loved the friends she had made in Pleasanton and liked living there, and it made no sense to her why her mother would want to move them again.

In September of 2001, several days before the move, the whole world stood still as Kay and millions watched the news and witnessed the nightmare of 9/11. Her heartbreak seemed so small compared to the pain she was watching unfold on television. But no matter how bad

138

she felt she kept herself busy with packing and daydreaming of her new life in Seattle.

The U-Haul truck Kay had rented was loaded, and Ben agreed to drive the truck and follow Kay in her car. He wanted to make sure they got to Seattle safely. He was annoyed that she felt the need to move in order to get over such a dirt bag, but he knew there was no stopping her once she had made up her mind. When they arrived at the apartment in Kirkland, he was impressed. He could not believe she had found a place so beautiful and with a view that even took his breath away. He immediately loved it there and vowed to visit often. Ben made her laugh harder than anyone, and he was just the friend she needed at the time. When she took him to the airport and said goodbye, she started crying, realizing she was all alone once again, with an angry little girl to boot.

* * *

Weeks turned into months, and she did the best she could to keep up her spirits, but moving to Seattle in September with a broken heart was not exactly the best way for Kay to snap out of her deep depression. Poor Lauren was doing her best to make new friends and get situated into a new school, only to come home each evening to a mother still in mourning over the biggest loser. She hated Ken for that and couldn't understand why her mother would bother grieving over a man who turned out to be a good riddance.

After several months of dark and lonely days, filled with nothing but nonstop tears and a reoccurring nightmare, Kay became so depressed she could not even go to work any longer. The new job was not what she had expected it to be, and she actually missed the Bay Area and the security of having Ben nearby.

In late December, Ben flew in for New Years. He spent the entire week making Kay laugh through her tears by teasing her about her heartbreak over the maintenance facility guy. She was in stitches with stomach cramps from laughing so much. It was a fun week. They took Lauren skiing, and when it came time for him to leave, Kay realized she had made a mistake and that her decision to move had been irrational.

On top of her angst over heartbreak, she now had a tremendous amount of regret about making the move and allowing such an asshole to infest her past and now her present. She had become a hopeless romantic, like she was stuck in some old black and white movie. There was no sun for months in Seattle, and her memories from that time were all in shades of gray. She finally called Ben in May and told him she was moving back to the Bay Area. She said she needed to stay with him until she found another job.

When Ben got that call, he was in shock. He thought she had lost her mind by moving Lauren there in the first place, and now she wanted to move again, after only nine months. He agreed, though, and before Kay sold all their furniture she broke the news to Lauren that they were returning to the Bay Area. Again, Lauren was distraught. She had made friends in Seattle and was enjoying living there, and now she had to start over again. She hated her mother with a passion for constantly uprooting her before she even had a chance to let her roots grow deep.

Lauren was so angry at her for moving them. That was a bad time! Lauren thought, and remembered being confused about why her mother moved them to Seattle to begin with.

Now, in reading her mother's private recollections, she was finally able to see the view from her mother's eyes. Her mother just wasn't able to cope with heartbreak at all. Her mother was depressed from all the bad things that happened during her childhood, her lifetime, and she simply could not suppress her feelings of depression any longer.

15

They moved back to the Bay Area and stayed with Ben for a month before Kay decided to settle into an apartment in San Jose. Kay never had a problem finding work, and within several weeks, she was rolling along in another sales position for Nextel, but she was not making nearly the money she had a year earlier. She met a young, hip group of people and felt comfortable for the first time in almost a year.

Meanwhile, Lauren settled into junior high and was hanging with an academic crowd. On the weekends Lauren always asked Kay to take her to the driving range so she could rent a bucket of balls to hit with her driver.

One Saturday as Kay was watching Lauren hit balls, she noticed an Asian man staring at Lauren, looming in the background and making comments about her swing. Then man looked at Kay and said, "She has a natural swing!"

Kay did not know the first thing about golf; she was only there to please Lauren. She felt uncomfortable and out of her league even being there. She answered, "I guess. That is what I have heard."

He asked Kay why Lauren did not have golf shoes or a glove, and Kay let him know she did not know she needed those things and that she did not have the money to buy them for her. When the man offered to buy them for Lauren since her mother could not afford them, Kay was offended and told the man that she would eventually get her the things she needed. He was a very calm, kind man and could see that Kay was upset, so he reassured her it was something he wanted to do. He let Kay know he had never seen a young girl with such a natural swing and could see that Lauren loved hitting the ball. He told Kay he had two daughters and would give anything if they were into golf like Lauren was.

As they talked, Kay discovered that he owned a coffee shop and had several businesses in Thailand. After they talked for a while he asked Kay to follow him in her car to a sporting goods store. She and Lauren were amazed that he was so interested in buying Lauren shoes and gloves, but Lauren was tickled and couldn't believe it was happening. He bought her the perfect pair of Callaway shoes and a glove that fit just right. Kay thanked the man over and over again and told him she wanted to pay him back, but he would not hear of it. He asked what Lauren's name was and told her he would watch for her to play in the LPGA someday. It was a magical day for Lauren, and she cried from pure happiness on the way home from the store.

Kay was equally amazed that day. She had heard from Ben and her father that Lauren had a natural swing, but for a complete stranger to say that and to invest in Lauren that way gave Kay the chills. She hoped someday Lauren would exceed in golf, but at the time she had money worries and needed to focus on paying the rent.

It had been years since Kay had money troubles, and it was a stressful time. All of the energy spent on the heartbreak over Ken had morphed into finding a way to make money.

They spent the next three years struggling financially in San Jose. Kay dated off and on, mainly losers, drinkers, and men of no real substance. Ben had met a woman named Mary, and they were engaged. Kay really liked Mary, and they all hung out on occasion. Kay's group of friends got together on the weekends. Life seemed to be flowing along in the social arena, but financially, it was becoming more and more difficult. It was expensive to live in the Bay Area, and her rent was a steep sixteen hundred a month.

Lauren had finished junior high with honors, but the high school Lauren was attending was not academically sound. Because of this, Kay began to think about where they could move within the Bay Area that might have a better public school for Lauren to attend. She wanted her to be safe and have the best academic education.

Kay was also beginning to realize she was going to be thirty-five and did not want to pay rent for the rest of her life, but she knew she would not be able to afford a home, condo, or an apartment in the Bay Area, for it was far too costly. She was thinking ahead, trying to figure out if moving somewhere else would be the best solution, a place where she could afford to buy a home and Lauren could thrive, get a decent education, and still play golf.

* * *

It was fall when Kay received a call from her mother telling her that her grandmother in Ohio had passed away. Over the years, Kay had been able to see her grandmother quite a bit, and she tried to fly back to Ohio every couple of years to visit her family.

Kay booked a flight to Ohio and flew out of San Jose, with one lay-over in Phoenix. As the plane descended into Phoenix, Kay looked down and noticed what seemed to be never-ending homes with pools. Kay had never thought of Phoenix as an option, but she believed everything happened for a reason, and she wondered if her grandmother wasn't trying to tell her something as the plane descended above all those houses. She had a feeling Phoenix might be a good place for her and Lauren—a place where she could transfer with her job and focus on building or buying a home. She thought it might be a dream she had given up on after Ken.

The idea of moving again infuriated Lauren, and she wondered how her mother could do that to her again. She was settled and had friends, and it didn't make sense to move her to another state where she knew nobody just to buy a home.

144

It was becoming too costly to live in the Bay Area, though, and Kay had taken advantage of everything there was to see there. She had spent years enjoying every bridge, beach, and city the Bay Area had to offer. She knew it would be difficult to leave, but she had to make a decision to either stay and continue to pay high rent just to sightsee or to finally buy a home for her and Lauren to settle in, a safe place where Lauren could attend high school and they could both lay down some roots.

Once she found out she could transfer her job to Phoenix, the decision was made. In Phoenix, Kay could actually afford a nice home with a pool, so she started making plans to move. She knew it would take several months, maybe up to six, to get things moving since she had her lease in San Jose and Lauren was still in school. Because she was house-shopping from some distance away, she figured the best way to do it was by looking at listings on the Internet.

Homes were selling like crazy in Phoenix at the time, and they were going up in price every day. It seemed as soon as Kay decided to move to Phoenix, the whole world wanted to as well. Suddenly she found herself in bidding wars for homes she had not even seen, and in the end, she was not able to buy, even with loan officers telling her to buy as soon as possible. Her money was tied up in her current apartment, and it was too risky. Even though everyone in Phoenix was doing it, Kay couldn't. She had very little extra income to take a risk like that.

Her plan was to leave in July, the hottest time of year in Phoenix. All she knew was that as each day passed, the pricing of the homes in Phoenix was skyrocketing, and Kay had to wait in order to move. There was nothing she could do but watch each day as homes kept going up and up in price, from one hundred thousand to one hundred and fifty thousand dollars within several months. There were moments when she considered backing out and just staying in California, but it was too late because her job had been filled. She had made her bed, and now she would

145

have to lie in it. To top it all off, she had heard there was a salesman that had the whole state of Arizona blocked off as his territory, and he was not happy about having to share his fortune with anyone. For Kay, again, things were starting to snowball out of control.

In the meantime, Lauren was throwing fits and sobbing about having to leave her friends in San Jose. She loved it there and did not want to leave, but Kay had already painted herself into a corner, and there was no way she could turn things around. She only hoped that playing golf in high school and living on or near a golf course would ease Lauren's pain.

Kay knew it would be a tough road ahead, but she had absolutely no idea how tough. The week before Lauren and she were set to move to Phoenix, the home Kay had in escrow fell through. She had no idea where they would live, and her whole reason for moving to Phoenix was no longer going to be a reality because they had no choice but to find an apartment to rent. She wanted so badly to finally have a home, and that was not happening. Prices had skyrocketed out of control in Phoenix, and she could not qualify for more than a one hundred thousand dollar loan with her salary. Nobody could buy a home in Phoenix for that unless it was in the ghetto, and she refused to lower her standards to that level. So, she rented an apartment that was near a golf course, in a good area with one of the best high schools in the state. She had to do something to right to the wrong, for she had made a grave decision in moving them there. To make matters worse, it was 118 degrees the day they arrived in Phoenix.

* * *

Lauren was miserable, and so was Kay. Ron, the guy at work who didn't want anyone to take over his territory, was also miserable, and he made it very clear that Kay's presence was not appreciated. She was in hell,

146

literal 120-degree hell! There was no turning around this time, though, and she had to make the best of it.

Ron did whatever he could to make Kay uncomfortable at work, including sexual harass her. He made sexual advances such as touching Kay's ass as she walked by. If she told him to stop, he denied he had done anything wrong and said she was crazy. It wasn't long before things spun out of control. Unlike the office where she worked in the Bay Area, this one was mostly men, a hardcore group of good ole' boys, so she was sorely outnumbered.

She finally grew so tired of Ron's remarks and advances that she had to contact Human Resources. She truly believed they would live up to their duty and help her, and she had no idea that the consequences of her choice would get her fired within a matter of months. Even though they reassured her that the discrimination and hostile work environment she reported would cease and that she would be able to work in a safe, non-hostile environment. However, that was not the case. In a matter of two months, Human Resources and the good ole' boys, along with the company, found a way to dismiss Kay. In order for them to avoid a lawsuit, they made sure to include her in part of a national layoff.

Discouraged, with no house, no job, and a bitter daughter, Kay was left with no options. She was given two months of severance pay, and Kay knew she had no choice but move on and accept the fact that it was her fault for complaining. She had to stay focused and figure out what to do next. Once again she just had to suck it up.

* * *

She regrouped and decided to focus on starting her own business. It was something she had dreamt of doing and had wanted to do for many years, but she never felt she could because she was a single mother and didn't want to risk instability. But the instability had set in, and she

147

was too tired to start over again. She took what little she had left and mustered it into becoming a recruiter like she had been in Salt Lake City.

It took her several months and a lot of sweat and tears, but finally Kay started making money—and good money at that. After some time, she was able to find and buy a condo near the high school Lauren attended.

For almost two years, Kay was able to build a small but successful business on her own. She took her sales experience and built some solid relations with several organizations, and that helped Kay to become financially secure and enabled her to get some enjoyment out of life. She had been raising Lauren on her own for fifteen years at this point and felt as if God was blessing her.

She was sure she was finally past the days of corporate America the good old' boys and all the abuse was behind her. There was no looking back. For the first time in her life, she had money in the bank, and there was no one telling her how or what to do. She didn't have to deal with men looking at her ass and making comments as she walked into an office each day, and she wasn't stuck in a cubicle. Kay vowed she would never put herself into that kind of environment or situation again.

She was enjoying the money and freedom, something she had never had much of. She went out and bought herself a BMW, and she was finally able to buy Lauren anything she needed, including a new set of new golf clubs. She also proudly bought her daughter a brand new bedroom set, along with a desk and computer. She wanted so badly to give Lauren everything she had promised her and more to make up for dragging her all over the place against her will.

Lauren recalled how angry she was at the time. She knew there was a strong possibility the next few pages in the notebook were going to sting. She took a deep breath and turned the page.

16

Kay had made some friends and was doing well in Phoenix, but no matter how hard she tried to feel at home there, she could not help but think and dream about the day Lauren would finally graduate so she could move back to California. She hated the dry heat in Phoenix, but she wasn't about to move Lauren again. She did her best to build up her business in hopes of making a move once her daughter went off to college.

Lauren was becoming a strong-willed teenager. She still visited Utah during the summers and usually returned with resentment and hostility toward her mother. Jesse's Grandmother had been bitter for years and could not seem to except the fact that Kay moving Lauren from Utah was the best thing for both, or so she had thought. It was easy for Lauren to believe her; she was an angry teen and hated her mother for moving her around so much. Lauren believed her mother to be unstable and accused her of not having her best interests at heart. Kay was constantly bashed by Jesse's Grandmother, and even her own family would concur at times that Kay was irrational especially after moving to Seattle after the break-up with Ken.

Lauren often accused her mother of ruining her life, and it was becoming clear to Kay that Lauren had started hanging out with the wrong crowd. Lauren found a job working at the local gym she was making money and seemed to be no longer interested in golf. She was becoming more and more distant and hard to handle.

In the midst of all of this, Kay had having a hard time focusing on her business, even though she was hanging onto to it the best she could. As the recession started to creep in, so did Lauren's bad behavior. While Kay was busy trying to keep her business alive, she was unable to see how much trouble her daughter was getting into—until the day the school called and asked her to come in and meet with them.

The principal let Kay know that Lauren was going to be released from the golf team for lying. She had been skipping classes and was caught in a lie trying to cover her tracks. Kay was livid to find this out and told the school officials that she had never had issues with Lauren in school. It was mind blowing to think Lauren had been tossed off the golf team, the most important thing in her young life.

When Kay and Lauren got home from that meeting, a huge argument ensued. Lauren blamed her mother and told her it was her fault that she had been kicked off the team; again, she told her mother she had ruined her life. Kay looked at her daughter with a raging stare and pounced on Lauren for being disrespectful.

Then came the words that would pierce Kay's heart forever. "I was raped!" Lauren screamed. "I was raped walking home from school!"

Kay dropped to her knees. She felt as though she had been hit by a bullet. The pain was so excruciating that it was as if the bullet entered her heart, like a knife being twisted in her chest. She could hardly breathe as she howled the words, "Oh my God! Oh my God!"

Lauren proceeded to tell her the whole story. "I was walking through the park after school, when suddenly I was pulled down into some bushes by my backpack. I struggled and screamed, but nobody was around. I kept fighting him off of me because he tried to rape me from behind. Because of my struggling, I ended up on my back with his forearm on my throat. I continued to cry for help, but he told me to shut up, and then he used his other hand to pull down my pants and rape me."

Kay screamed out in a pain so intense it could only be second to the death of one's child. She felt sharp, prominent pain in her chest as Lauren continued.

Lauren described the man in detail, right down to what he was wearing. "He was a Black man with golden eyes," she said.

Kay's whole body ached, and she moaned with every word she was hearing.

"He was wearing khaki shorts and a white t-shirt, and as soon as he was done with me, he got up and ran. I barely remember getting up and walking home." Lauren said, "I did not tell anyone. I wanted to pretend it never happened." She had inherited that trait from her mother.

Kay crawled over to Lauren and started hugging her and rocking her in her arms, crying and screaming, "No, no! Not my baby! Not my baby!" She asked her when it all happened, but before she heard her answer, Kay said she was going to call the police.

Lauren cried out, "No! No! It was six months ago, and that is why I did not want you to know. I want to just forget about it. I don't need you freaking out about me. No, Mom!"

Kay yelled back, "We have to, baby! We have to! Do you want this man to keep doing this? What if there are other girls? Maybe the police already know who he is. Maybe they're looking for him. Please, baby! We have to call. We just have to. I know it's going to be hard, but that son of a bitch...oh my God!" Kay broke down, weaker than ever, crying and pleading at the same time for Lauren to understand. "He has already affected your life. You are not the same person. You are failing at school and can't even play golf, something you loved. We have to try. Please, Lauren. I am calling the police."

Kay had always believed she had been protecting Lauren and giving her a better life by moving her around to different cities. She always made sure the school districts were the best in the area before choosing exactly where to settle down. Most of all, she avoided Utah and Jesse like the plague. But now, her wanting things to be better had led to her baby getting raped and that thought nearly destroyed her. No other pain she had experienced—

not even seeing her father kill himself—was as painful as knowing her only child had been so brutally attacked. She wanted to find and kill the man who did it, and she vowed to do the best she could to help police find him so he could be brought to justice, whether or not Lauren liked it or not.

She soon found out that contacting the police was a lost cause. They had no way of finding the man and had no evidence even if they did. The police told Kay that other girls had been attacked in months prior, but all were Laurens age, and they never reported anything until after the evidence had already been washed away. They had a description of the man but no solid leads.

Kay had to learn to live with the guilt of her daughter's rape. It was torture, and it would haunt her for the rest of her life. Moving them to Phoenix was the biggest mistake she had ever made, and she could not wait to leave, but she had no idea how or exactly when she would be able to. For months, Kay walked the park at night, the place where Lauren was raped. She carried a container of mace and knife in a tight grip. She thought to herself, *come on you motherfucker! Come and rape me!* She was starting to go crazy with rage and unanswered revenge. She wanted to kill him and hoped he would return. Night after night, she walked there, hoping he would dare hop out of the bushes and try to attack her. She believed it would make things all better if she caught him and ended his life.

By the time Lauren finished reading the last sentence on the page, she was crying at the thought of her mother walking through the park, brandishing a knife in hopes of killing the son of a bitch that had robbed her of her virginity. She had been reading for hours and hoped her mother had not written about other hurtful moments of her life. She skipped through that part quickly, speed reading over it because the details were simply too much for her to handle. That time in her life was a blur, and she did not want to relive those moments, much in the same way her mother never spoke of witnessing her own father's suicide. Wow, she thought, sobbing in the back of the plane and trying not to draw attention to herself, I'm more like Mom than I thought.

What struck her the most was just how much her mother loved her. She had a newfound respect and love for her, she knew what she was about to read would be even more difficult now that she understood her mother on a deeper level.

She was contemplating closing the notebook, she knew her past better than her mother did and wasn't sure if she wanted to read her mother's version. But she continued on.

17

It was a Saturday evening; several weeks after Lauren had finally confessed to her rape and had to meet with the police. She still hated her mother for calling them. Lauren came home and had been badly beaten. Kay was mortified and immediately tried to help, but Lauren was stoned out of her mind and pushed Kay away, stumbled into her room, slammed the door, and locked it behind her.

Kay was freaked out, for Lauren had never pushed her mother before, and to make matters worse, she was suspicious of her being drunk or using drugs like her loser of a father. She noticed Lauren's backpack sitting on the kitchen table and started to go through it. That was when she found the sandwich bag, with something a bit more volatile in it than peanut butter and jelly; it was a quarter of the way full of cocaine. She was immediately confused and angry. She started banging on Lauren's door, demanding her to open it. Kay had always tried to teach Lauren to avoid drugs, because of Jesse's past. It was Kay's worst nightmare that she would become like him. Lauren had promised, saying she would never touch drugs, so finding the cocaine in her bag was a nightmare.

When Lauren did finally open her bedroom door, she hit Kay and knocked her to the floor. She snatched the cocaine from Kay's hand and told Kay to stay away from her.

Kay ran to her phone and began to dial the police.

As she was dialing, Lauren threatened her and told her, "If you call them, I'll tell them you beat me and I was just protecting myself!"

Alone and with no other family in Phoenix, Kay went into shock and did not know what to do. It was one o'clock in the morning, and she did not have anyone she could call on.

When Lauren ran out the door, Kay had no idea where she was going. She only believed that Lauren would call the police on her and put the blame on her because she was so angry at her mother. She also was worried about Lauren's reputation and if she were to call the police it could ruin Laurens life forever.

Kay was frantic and went to call Mark and Suzanne; then remembered they were in Europe on vacation and wouldn't be returning for another week. She called everyone she could praying someone would answer and give her some guidance. When she did finally did hear back from her friends, they said there was nothing they could do. They told her to just let Lauren go and it would work itself out or to call the police.

Her stepsister Sheri and stepbrother Vance lived in Texas, and she rarely saw them. Her brother Luke had married and moved back to Ohio. She was all alone in Arizona. There were many times that she missed Richard and this was one of them, she knew if he was alive she would never have felt so alone. She needed his strength and wisdom now and more than ever.

Losing her daughter to drugs was beyond her comprehension. Lauren had always been such a good kid, until the rape ruined her life. Kay felt like everything she had been living for was gone, just like that, the night her daughter walked out that door, stoned, beaten, and hating her mother.

Several days passed when Kay was able to finally find Lauren. She had fallen so far into using drugs that her only recourse was to lie and stay in a place where she could use without being questioned. So, she went to live with her friend Bonnie. At Bonnie's place, she could use drugs and alcohol without anyone suspecting a thing. Everyone just thought Lauren was a sweet, innocent child, and Bonnie's mother allowed Lauren to stay with them and believed every lie Lauren told her about Kay being a horrible parent and beating her. Because of the lies Lauren told her about Kay, Bonnie's mother would not allow Kay to come near Lauren. To make matters worse for Kay, Bonnie's mom worked for Child Protective Services, and she wholeheartedly believed Lauren's bruised and scraped-up face was due to Kay. She even was in the midst of helping Lauren complete the paperwork to become emancipated so she would never have to live under her mother's roof or rules again. It was a nightmare for Kay, unimaginable to a parent concerned and begging for help for her child.

Kay had become so desperate, and she had nowhere to turn. With all other options exhausted save suicide, she did the unthinkable and called Jesse's Grandmother. It was her very last resort, and she had sunken so low she was barely breathing. All she could think about was getting Lauren out of Arizona, away from the place where she'd been raped and where she'd started using drugs. Kay began to believe Lauren and Jesse's Grandmother was right; she had ruined Lauren's life.

Jesse had been in jail after being busted with drugs several years earlier. Kay had heard he was finally clean but figured it wasn't true. Regardless of the issues between them, Kay knew Jesse's Grandmother truly loved Lauren, and she could only cling to the small shred of hope that she might be able to save her, especially once she heard about Lauren's drug use. She would have never stood helplessly by and let Lauren turn into a druggie or an alcoholic.

Kay made the hardest call of her life and asked Jesse's Grandmother for help. She told Kay she would help her and that she would send Jesse to Arizona to pick Lauren up. Kay agreed reluctantly. Jesse had no money. He was divorced and had been living off of different woman, ten bucks here and twenty there, for years. Now Kay had to rely on him to use his grandmother's car and money and hope that Jesse would come directly to Arizona to help.

It took days for him to get there, and it felt like years for Kay. When he arrived, he checked into a hotel near Kay's condo. Jesse called Kay and told her he needed to rest from the long twelve-hour drive and that they would be leaving soon for Utah. Kay found it odd because she had driven straight through from Phoenix to Salt Lake City and back many times alone and had never needed two or three days to recover. She had a sneaking suspicion something was wrong, that maybe she had made things worse by calling his Grandmother, but she hung onto hope because it was all she had left.

Kay went Lauren's school to have her released so she could attend school in Utah. Finally, after three days of Jesse screwing around, he called to tell Kay he had Lauren and that they were finally leaving. He assured her they would be in Utah the following evening.

In the meantime, Kay had been packing her own bag. She had plans to drive to Utah. She planned to find a small apartment there, one she could stay in so she could be close in case Lauren needed her. She was somewhat relieved to see that things were finally moving along, and she hoped things would be better for Lauren once she got away from the home she had been living in and the woman who believed her every lie.

Kay drove straight through the night to her parents' house in Kaysville and arrived around eleven o'clock in the morning. She knew Lauren would be arriving that evening. Throughout the trip, Jesse texted Kay and told her everything was fine and they would be arriving in Utah soon.

Kay's parents had just arrived home from Europe and were completely shocked to see Kay at their door step. They were even more surprised at how frail, tired, and old she looked. She was as surprised as they were. She was going to use their spare key to stay at there place until they returned, she had no idea they would be home.

They could see how pain had completely devoured Kay. But Kay noticed that they both looked tired and sick themselves. They had come home a day earlier from

Europe due to a bad case of food poisoning, they were both very tired and very ill.

Once they were made abreast of what was happening they were as anxious as Kay to know that Lauren had arrived safely and they were worried about the fact Jesse was involved. But she told them that his Grandmother swore he would help get her back to Utah and they would all work together to get her into rehab.

Hours passed by, Kay sent a text to Jesse to see where they were. Strangely, his responses became slower and slower, and he eventually started avoiding her texts and calls altogether.

That evening, Kay looked at her parents, who were watching television and said, "I know something is wrong. I have a really strong feeling Jesse does not have Lauren— that he left her back there in Phoenix."

Kay's parents told her she was just going crazy due to the tremendous stress and made her go to bed.

As Kay lay in bed, her mind was spinning. She could not sleep. She made a decision to call Lauren's workplace and ask for her, just to see what they would say. She dialed the number, hoping to hear, "She no longer works here."

Someone picked up the phone and said, "Hello. Life Lite Fitness. Can I help you?"

Kay replied, "Yes. Can I speak with Lauren?"

The voice on the other end of the phone said, "Hold on one minute, and I will get her. I think she just walked back into the locker room."

Kay immediately hung up the phone, ran into the living room where her father was still watching television, and cried out, "He left her there! He left her there!"

Mark immediately sat up and looked at Kay as if she had really lost her mind. He asked "How do you know?"

Kay said, "I called her work, and they said she was in the locker room!"

Kay's assumptions were right, because Jesse did leave Lauren in Phoenix, once again proving his worthlessness and making things a hundred times worse. That was something he was good at.

Kay immediately grabbed her things and ran out of her parents' house. Mark chased after her and told her she needed sleep before making the twelve-hour drive back to Phoenix. Mark knew Kay too well and knew she would drive straight through the night alone. Kay heeded his advice and went back into the house, took a sleeping pill, and cried herself to sleep.

The next morning, she woke, immediately grabbed her stuff, jumped in the car, and raced back to Arizona. She had crisscrossed the western deserts so many times before, but this was by far her most memorable drive. She sobbed as if her daughter had died. She thought she would run out of tears once she hit Las Vegas, but she had no such luck. As she drove through Vegas and headed over the Hoover Dam, she knew she still had 250 more miles of dark, vast Arizona desert to go. A random truck passing her in the night was her only company, and she cried out to God to help her save Lauren and to keep her from driving off the road.

Lauren felt sick; she knew she been such a shit. Wow! I hated her so my mother so much during that time. But she didn't give up on me...If I were I would have! She wanted so badly to call her mother right then and apologize but that was not an option. So she asked the flight attendant for another drink.

18

Kay somehow made it through the last two hundred miles and was able to drag herself to her bed, where she slept for twelve hours straight. The depression and fatigue made it almost impossible for her to wake up.

A knock on her door was what ultimately made her get out of bed. She cracked open the door, sure she was going to find a traveling salesperson or some kind of religious people trying to give her a pamphlet.

"Hello," said the woman at the door. "Are you Kay?"

Kay replied, "Yes. Can I help you?"

The woman answered, "I am with CPS, and—"

Kay interrupted "What is CPS?"

"Child Protective Services."

"What?"

"Yes, ma'am. Your ex-husband called to report abuse against your daughter Lauren."

Kay started to get dizzy and felt herself fall back against the wall. When she regained her footing a bit, she figured she may as well be hospitable. "Please come in and sit. Is it okay if I smoke?" Kay slinked down to the floor holding her head in hands. She asked the woman, "Did you know my daughter was raped?"

"No," the woman responds.

Kay got up and walked over to the desk where she kept letters and papers concerning Lauren, her schoolwork as well as the police report. She picked up the pile and started shaking it at the woman and yelling at her, "This is what child abuse looks like! A parent being abused by their only child, a child that is so gone on drugs she has the nerve to lie about the mother that is trying so desperately to help her. To top it off, her alcoholic loser father who has never done anything to help me raise Lauren calls CPS, and tells them I'm an abusive parent! Well, first of all he is not my ex-husband! And if I am such an abusive parent, then why in the hell would Jesse leave his only child with me?"

Not only had she been beaten up by her own child, but now she was being questioned about being a bad parent and beating Lauren—something she would absolutely never do. She thought she had been hurt enough, but apparently the hurt had just begun.

The woman began spouting to Kay the version she was told, which had been a complete fabrication made up by Jesse. He wanted out, and what better way than to leave his child with a woman who believed her lies and by calling CPS? The CPS woman believed Kay after looking at all the paperwork and recommended that Kay call the police again, as well as a counselor.

Once the woman left, Kay did her best to pull herself together. She wanted to kill Jesse, and if she had been in the same state or even within one hundred miles of him, she would have hunted him down and done just that. Thoughts of taking a bat and bashing his brains in kept running through her head. He was a sick asshole and did nothing but take up space on a planet already saturated with garbage. She had nobody left to cry to and or to help her, so she resorted to taking some sleeping pills, lying down on the floor right where she sat, and falling into a deep sleep.

She woke up every few hours and took more pills in order to keep sleeping. After four days of nothing but sleep, she crawled into a hot shower. She wondered how she was still breathing. She was dead emotionally, and it seemed almost ridiculous to her that she would feel hungry enough to want to eat. But weak and frail, she drove to the grocery store. She knew she was going broke, so as she slowly pushed the shopping cart around, she had the feeling she was practicing becoming a homeless person. She put only a few items in her cart: a sandwich, bag of chips, and a bottle of wine. She was going through

163

motions, but none of them made sense. Her subconscious was doing all the work. She was relieved to not have a job at the time; she would not have survived being fired and losing her daughter at the same time. Losing her business was a private issue, and nobody needed to know. It gave her time to grieve.

She began running out of money and had to make a decision about keeping her condo or letting it go, which seemed to be the answer. It seemed a moot point to try to hold on to anything.

Three weeks passed, and she received a call from a police officer letting her know that Lauren had been arrested for stealing at a local grocery. Kay told him to take her to jail, but the police officer insisted she come and pick her up at the store. She went with her camera and made the officer open the door of the police car so she could take pictures of Lauren handcuffed; she wanted to send the photos in case of any problems CPS, Jesse or his Grandmother.

The police let her know that Lauren would have to go to court. As Lauren sat in the police car calling Kay a "fucking bitch," Kay let the officer know what Lauren had put her through and that she did not want to take her home.

He looked at Lauren and started yelling, "You better shut the fuck up! Don't you ever talk to your mother that way again! If you were my kid, I would beat the shit out of you, so I give your mom permission to do the same, and I will stand behind her 100 percent."

* * *

Kay did not want to take Lauren home. She was disgusted with her and frankly did not want to be abused any longer—or to be accused of it. Lauren finally got her wake-up call. She went home with Kay, but the two did not talk for weeks. Even though Kay knew Lauren was safe, the damage had already been done. She was so wounded and scarred by what had happened; she did the best she could to stop feeling angry and to stop the financial destruction that Lauren's misbehaviors had caused.

Lauren went to court and was given probation and told that the charge would be dropped when she turned eighteen if she were to stay out of trouble.

Unfortunately, it was a time when the whole country was getting ready to experience financial setbacks. The failing real estate market had hit Arizona especially hard, and widespread fear was starting to set in. Kay had already lost her condo and was struggling to make ends meet in a place she found to rent.

She was contacted by a company based in New York. They had heard of Kay through one of their business partners and asked her if she would be willing to work for them and she could telecommute. It would be a steady income and the timing was perfect. All Kay cared about was getting back on her feet again financially. Something she had become so good at.

* * *

Kay started to make some progress financially until October of that year when the stocks tanked. The company in New York had set up a conference call for all their nationwide representatives to let them know the company was going to have to cut back and could only keep their New York based employees onboard. Kay was offered a job if she moved there, but she couldn't leave Lauren.

Lauren had begun golfing again, and as far as Kay knew she was doing well, though they rarely communicated. Lauren had been pulling her own life and reputation together by spending every spare minute she had at the golf course, trying to make up for lost time. She knew everybody at the local Golf course, and the golf Pro for the course saw such big potential in her that he worked

165

with her for free. Lauren was shooting a little above par, and she still had until June before she would graduate high school. She was becoming a better golfer, and colleges and universities began to take notice when she played in the Junior Golf Association and the Arizona State championship.

Kay wasn't sure if she would be playing golf for Arizona State or Mesa Junior College or leaving Arizona altogether since Lauren began getting offers to play golf all over the country. She was aware that Lauren had a strong passion for golf and wanted to be recognized nationally. It was important for Lauren to get a full-ride scholarship with living expenses, because if she were to leave Arizona, Kay couldn't afford to pay for her housing out of state. Kay tried her best to keep track, but Lauren did everything in her power to keep her life to herself and keep her mother in the dark about it.

While Lauren's golf game was improving, her attitude remained bitter and nasty toward Kay. It wasn't easy for Kay, and she became so tired of Lauren's bullshit that all she could do was focus more and more on her own life. She realized it would not be long before Lauren would be eighteen, and then she would be free to do whatever she wanted to. Even though she was fed up with Lauren, she still loved her very much.

As far as Kay was concerned, moving them to Phoenix had admittedly been the biggest mistake of her life next to allowing Jesse back into hers and Lauren's lives when she was a baby and going bananas after Ken left her for another woman. The life Lauren was creating by playing golf helped take some of the pain away from their four hellish years in Phoenix. Kay could not wait to leave Arizona.

Lauren laid her head back on the seat and closed her eyes. She knew she had put her mother through more than anyone deserved. She had been a total bitch to her and had tried to keep her at a distance all through her junior and senior years in high school, no matter how much her mother tried to be a part of her life, but she resented her mother for moving her around.

She felt sick about what she had done and, really hated reading about it, especially since she had blocked out so much of it in order to move on. She hadn't realized back then just exactly how much it affected her mother, and she had never known the deep hurt her mother had endured.

She decided to take a break. She needed time to regroup and was getting tired, so she dozed off for two hours.

When she woke, she realized it would be another two hours before she arrived in New York. She figured she would continue reading. She convinced herself that she had already read what had to have been the worst of it.

19

An old friend named David had flown into Phoenix on business, and he and Kay always had lunch when he was in town. Six years earlier, Kay had helped David nail down a job at Stayton Metals. That company had been bought out by CMT Corporation, and he was now a district manager. He had worked his way up and was still living in the Bay Area. He kept in touch with Kay and always told her he felt grateful for her helping him land a job when he desperately needed one. It was because of her that he was able to be in the position he was in.

David had always wanted to someday do something to pay Kay back for her referral. While they were having lunch, Kay mentioned to David that Phoenix had been rough. She told him she wished she had never left the Bay Area, but Lauren still had six months left before graduating, and she had to stay in Phoenix until she knew what Lauren's college plans were. He mentioned to Kay that the Phoenix division of his company was hiring, but she was leery because metals sales is a male-dominated industry, and she didn't need a repeat of the past. It made her uneasy, but she needed the money.

About a week later, David contacted her and let her know that a man named Mauricio would be in touch and that the position was basically hers if she wanted it. David also let her know that a man by the name of Dale Shrake was going to be starting the following week in the same sales position as Kay. Dale Shrake was a creep, and David knew it and wanted to warn her. "Watch out for Mauricio," he told her since he really liked Mauricio and knew that Dale would try to take his job.

Kay thanked him and let him know she would call him once she met with Mauricio, but the truth was, Kay was bothered by what she had heard from David. She had known Dale and seen him at different conventions when she was working for Daly, Inc. She knew he was a bit creepy and that he was one of those guys who seemed to think he was better than everyone. He was a control freak, and he was always in charge of training and presenting. She remembered how he enjoyed embarrassing someone if they were not looking directly at him the whole time he was speaking. She could not wait to get to the airport once the training courses he held were through. The memories were blurry, but they gave her a bad feeling. She just had to remind herself that he was not going to be her manager. He would be doing the exact job as her, selling in his own territory. She found it a bit odd that he had a job so low on the totem pole, but at least that meant she could stay away from him since they were on equal levels, even if he didn't think so.

She was contacted by Mauricio, and David was right about the position, because Mauricio made it sound as if Kay would be starting the following week. Kay had to tell him she needed to understand what she would be selling, as well as salary and benefits, before making up her mind. Mauricio set up a time to meet several days later, and upon meeting him, she felt confident that she would be okay working for him.

It was no wonder David liked Mauricio. He seemed to be a kind man and had been a manager for several years. She could tell he was about five to ten years younger than her, and he seemed nervous. She reassured him that she only wanted to be a sales representative and had no aspirations of becoming a manager. He made her an offer, and she accepted and started work the following week.

She felt comfortable right away and thought that after her orientation with Human Resources, everything would be great. She hoped this would be the fresh start she had been wanting for so long. She felt she had a chance to have some security and was blessed to have a decent job during a recession. She only had one concern: she had a weird feeling about seeing Dale Shrake again. Kay could see a psychopath approaching from miles away. She hoped she was wrong about him and that he'd changed since she knew him before, but as it turned out, her gut was right on the money.

As Mauricio walked her around to meet all the people on his team, she saw Dale. He immediately got up and was so loud and over-the-top nice. It was more awkward than she had expected. When Mauricio left her to fill out paperwork for her laptop and company cell phone, Dale whispered to her, "Come here."

She looked at him strangely and looked around to see why he was whispering.

He waved his hand, motioning for her to come to him again, and said, "Come here."

She walked over to him cautiously. When he pulled her into a small conference room, she asked, "What are you doing? What do you want?"

In a snake-like fashion, he whispered to her, "We are here to clean up the mess that Mauricio has made with his team."

She looked alarmed and said, "What?"

He continued, "Nobody likes Mauricio, and I have been told by Kim, the regional manager, that they want to replace him. I know she wanted us here in order to help get the sales team on track and Mauricio out."

Kay looked dumbfounded as she responded, "I don't know what you are talking about, but I was hired to sell and that is all. I am not here to be part of any political takedown. I just want to do my job."

He continued, "Oh, I know. I understand, but I have let the others know we are here to clean things up. They don't like Mauricio either."

Kay was mortified. She had just finished her first day of orientation, and she knew he might be trouble, but this was too much. She was instantly offended that he would include her in anything that had to do with getting someone demoted. She felt ill. She opened the conference room door to make sure nobody actually saw her in there with him. She told him she wanted to be left alone to do her job. She despised him and had only been in the building for three hours, and her worst fear was coming true. *God*! she thought to herself. *Why? Why can't I just have a peaceful life and go to work and do my job without weirdoes and drama?* She was so pissed off and hoped nobody had seen her talking to the clown. He was slimy and belonged on a used car lot. He was fidgety and just made her uncomfortable and queasy. His every intention was to become manager, and Kay would not support him no matter what. David had been right about him, but she did not think she would find out on her first day just how right he was.

Having now experienced all types of arrogant, insecure men that would do anything to make sure Kay would not outshine them, her instincts were telling her to quit. Dale was clearly going to be more trouble than she had signed up for, but she needed the money, and she believed with her experience that she could handle anything. But the thought of Dale ever being her manager made her physically ill.

Dale pretended to know everything, but he had no intention of selling one damn thing. The only thing on his mind was taking over Mauricio's position as manager over the sales team. Mauricio had some issues with talking down to people, so the rest of the team thought it was exciting that someone was coming in "to make things right." Dale thought he was the man, and Kay thought he was a piece of shit. Kay knew he had one thing on his mind, and that was to control woman. He was a lonely, creepy son of a bitch. She began having flashbacks, recalling how he constantly talked about woman. He was fifty-two and admitted to living with his parents. He was very tall and very white, almost an albino. What little hair he had was white, and he had a serial killer eyes. She remembered she had heard from some woman in the past that he made her uncomfortable, and she began to have more memories of him and others' experiences with him.

The main thing she remembered was always feeling lucky when she was able to get on a plane and leave the area he was in. It was barely tolerable back then to stomach him, and things hadn't changed much.

The more Kay tried to avoid Dale, the more he leered at her. He seemed quite obsessed with getting her attention and wanting to be close to her. She could tell he was becoming more obsessed by the day, but she couldn't understand why. As always, she pretended everything was alright and dug her heels in for her job. She had made a sale within her first week, and she immediately began to sense envy and resentment coming from Dale. She did her best to purposely avoid him, and she was rarely in the office because she was in the field selling.

After several weeks of completely avoiding him and ignoring his phone calls, Kay was finally cornered by him in the warehouse. He started talking to her about Mauricio, and the whole time he was talking, he was pinning her into a space between a wall and a shelf. She suddenly realized she could not move; he was towering over her and talking nonsense. She started to feel trapped, sick, and queasy. She felt he just wanted to be near her and was try to intimidate her at the same time. Kay started to have difficulty breathing, and suddenly she snapped and yelled as loud as she could, "Leave me alone!" She tried to push him out of the way while yelling, "Don't you ever pull me into an area and corner me again! God, just leave me alone!"

When she tried to run, he grabbed her arm and said, "I know about your past and you complaining to Human Resources at Daly, Inc."

She was in shock that he had grabbed her. She pulled away from him and screamed, "Stay the fuck away from me!"

Kay was petrified and called David to tell him what had happened. David was not amused and felt bad for Kay. He thought Dale was a scum bag, but David was a manager himself, and he did not want trouble. He was doing his best to be supportive and politically correct at the same time. He told her to stay away from him and to just keep doing a good job. "You're already being noticed for selling right out of the gate," he said. "You just need to ignore that asshole and keep working. Eventually you'll be able to transfer to another office, hopefully in California, as soon as she knew what Lauren's plans would be after graduating."

In the meantime, she really hoped someone had witnessed what he had done to her, but there were no cameras or people around the area where he had put her in such a compromising position. He was not only obsessed with Kay, but he was becoming more and more insanely jealous. She was already outshining him and had no intention of helping him self-promote. She even made it a point to proclaim how much she liked Mauricio, right in front of her co-workers and Dale himself.

Every time Kay saw Dale, he was talking about how he and Kay had been brought in to overthrow Mauricio and change things. Kay constantly reassured the team that he was full of it and that was not true. She reiterated time and time again to anyone who would listen that she wanted nothing to do with whatever Dale was planning. All she wanted to do was sell.

Kay learned her job and work closely with another team member named Maria. After a few weeks, Kay and Maria were doing very well. They made a good team and managed to land some meetings with large accounts, resulting in great success for them and for the company at large. Kay was acknowledged by Mauricio and his manager Mike for doing such a great job.

* * *

It was a Monday morning when Kay got the bad news that Mauricio had been let go and Dale would be her new manager. Immediately, Kay called David and let him know that she wanted to quit. He told her to hang on because it would only be a matter of months before Kay would be able to transfer.

Kay voiced her concerns to Maria, and the pit in her stomach kept growing with each passing day. She knew it was going to be hell, but she did not have a choice; she could either grin and bear it or quit. She chose to keep selling in order to eventually move on.

Within several days, Dale demanded that Kay get into his car to go to lunch. She told him she had an appointment, but when he offered to go with her, she blatantly refused. He was frustrated; she had already built a good reputation in just the few months she had been there, so he was not able to go to his manager and complain about her.

Clever as he was, though, he found a way to get to her and try to ruin her reputation. He began retaliating by sabotaging her work and telling people she was high maintenance. Dale started to contact accounts she was working on, and this made a mess of things. It was all part of his obsession, his plan to make her quit and ruin her reputation. He was so desperate and lonely, and Kay felt like he was taking her rejection the way a scorned lover would. He was a sociopath, a psychopath, and a narcissist all rolled into one, and he was starting to scare the shit out of her. She was determined she could overcome anything, including a creep like him.

Once again, she had been having more than just the nightmare of that fatal night when her father killed Gina and then himself. She even began to have flashbacks of it during the day as well. Pictures would pop up in her head of what she had seen: Gina's blood, her lying on the floor, and her father with his head blown off. She started to feel the same fear she had felt as a child when her father came home and bullied her and made her feel like a nobody. All the drama with Dale was just stirring up memories of another monster in her life.

Lauren finally came to Kay for advice about where she should attend college. She had three offers and was confused about what to do: one from Mesa Junior College, one from Oregon State, and one from Penn State. All the offers were full-ride scholarships with living quarters included, and that only made the decision more difficult.

Lauren's main concern was whether or not she was ready to move out of Arizona. It was scary for her, and even though she resented her mother, she had been her lifeline. Kay let her know that no matter her decision, she would support and love her no matter what, and she was extremely proud of her accomplishments. Lauren had really pulled it back together academically. She was at the top of her class, and she had regained her status as a golf phenomenon.

Finally, Lauren decided on Penn State and began making plans to leave in the fall. Kay was emotional about her daughter moving so far away, as any mother would be, but she wanted her daughter to succeed and had secretly hoped she would choose to leave Arizona. She had mixed feelings like any parent with a child ready to go off to college.

* * *

By June, Kay knew she still had several more months to hang on before she could transfer. Lauren would be with her until late August, and she couldn't begin the process until then. It was difficult to wait because things at work were becoming more and more volatile, and Dale was pushing her buttons in hopes that she would get mad enough to quit. He did everything he could to separate her and Maria. He hated the fact that they were causing such a commotion in the office; they were doing a great job, and people were constantly commenting on their accomplishments. This had Dale seething with jealousy.

175

Kay had been putting together information that would help the estimators in the office bid some big projects. If they managed to land the contracts, it would mean a huge bonus for Kay. She found out that Dale had told the estimators that they would not need to bid the work because he had spoken to the customers, and they were not happy with Kay. This outraged Kay to no end. She was at the end of her rope, but she didn't know what she could do about it. There wasn't anyone she could complain to, as she knew nobody would listen. So she lashed out and Dale and told him once again to stay the hell away from her and to stop sabotaging her work. This time she put it in an email so she could show anyone in case he kept doing things to make her look bad. Sadly, he got off on knowing he had gotten to Kay, and it just made him want to be more creative in coming up with ways to screw with her and her work.

Everything he did was underhanded, and he was a bully, plain and simple. He continued to tell the other men in the office she was high maintenance, which meant when Kay needed something, she was avoided or ignored. He was making it next to impossible for her to do her job, and that made it difficult for her to transfer. Her reputation was being ruined. She had done everything she could to avoid saying anything to anyone about it, but when he did the unthinkable, she had no choice.

It was a Wednesday, a scorching 118-degree day in late June. She had at an appointment, and just as she was leaving it, she saw Dale standing at the door as she walked out of the building. She was so startled that she screamed. She asked him what in the hell he was doing there.

In the creepiest voice he could muster, which wasn't hard for him, he replied, "I'm your boss."

She was confused and couldn't believe he was trying to scare her.

He continued, "I am supposed to follow you around and know what you are doing at all times. I watch

176

you, and I know where you live. I know everything about you, Kay."

She started freaking out and yelling in the middle of the parking lot, "Stay away from me, you psychopath!"

He laughed.

She ran to her car and drove away quickly. She made sure he was nowhere behind her by taking side streets and driving as quickly as possible in order to hide her car and pull over. She started crying out of pure fear, a fear she had not felt for almost twenty-five years. *Why is he doing this to me?* She came to the conclusion that he really wanted to scare or upset her so badly she would quit. She was determined not to, and she drove straight to the office in tears and went to talk to Mike, the psychopath's manager.

She explained everything to Mike: the warehouse incident, him sabotaging her work and telling everyone she was high maintenance, and how he had followed her and told her she knew where she lived. Mike stared at her like she was crazy, and clearly, she could see that Dale had brainwashed everyone, Mike included. She was upset, and in a man's world, that meant she was high maintenance.

Mike told her he would get Human Resources involved because there was nothing he could do for her. She told him she did not want that because she did not want to lose her job for complaining—that all she wanted was to just do her job without being harassed and bullied by her manager.

Mike said, "I know about your past. You were complaining about some men at your last job."

Kay was mortified and rendered speechless. She got up to walk out of his office and turned back around. Standing in Mike's doorway she said the words, "He is going to do something really bad, and you are going to regret believing anything that psychopath has had to say."

After that, she left the office and went home. She cried herself to sleep and did not know what to do. She knew she had ruined her chances of ever being relocated—

no, Dale had ruined them. She was so afraid of him, though, and she had no choice but to issue a complaint since she didn't know how far he was willing to go to get her to quit.

She was soon contacted by a woman in Human Resources, and Kay went ahead and told the woman everything. The lady asked if Kay had any proof or witnesses, but all Kay had was the email telling him to leave her alone. After supposedly talking to Dale, the HR lady and the company as a whole found no reason to believe Kay, or at least they didn't want to admit what was going on right under their corporate noses.

Kay was devastated. Once again, nobody would listen to her, and she had to shut up and concede to the control of madman or quit. She had no choice, as the job was her only livelihood, and she was stuck there until she could find something else. There was no way she was going to quit her job and be poor because some sick son of a bitch wanted her to. She was labeled a complainer and an outcast. She was no longer a shining star, but a troublemaker. Dale's plan was working, and he had everything under his control—including Kay. Kay had his number, though, and she knew he was going to ruin and harass her as much as possible. He was a disgusting, pathetic, lonely psychopath. Kay had known he was trouble, but he was far worse than she could have possibly imagined.

It wasn't long before David called Kay. He had heard the news that she had finally broken down and complained, but he had no idea just how bad it had become. He was disappointed in her, and she knew she no longer had the option of relocating now that the report from Human Resources had been written making her look like a drama queen and an instigator.

She decided to seek legal advice. She met with an attorney, and he told her he needed to see a copy of the report from Human Resources. She gave him the report, and he told her to go downtown to the Equal Employment

Opportunity Commission (EEOC) and file a charge with them. He told her it would take some time, but by filing a report with the EEOC, CMT would not be able to fire her without a damn good reason. He said he would take her case in a heartbeat if the EEOC found that she had been harassed. He also told her to start recording and sending emails to Human Resources and management each and every time Dale did anything that made her uneasy.

* * *

As Kay sat on the freeway onramp getting ready to join rush-hour traffic, she could not hold back her tears. As they rolled down her face, she knew the time had come—the time she had been anticipating for the last nineteen years. Her little Lauren was leaving, going off to college. She had received the news just a few days after the unfortunate events had unfolded at work. She felt trapped by her lease; she still had three months left. As she inched along in the snail's pace freeway traffic, waiting her turn to merge, she could not believe what was happening. Once again, she had learned the hard way that she had no safety in Human Resources or anywhere in corporate America, and now she had to drive around knowing Dale was following her around and knew where she lived. She was angry and terrified, but there wasn't anything she could do. She had no proof; it was her word against his.

Her life had been nothing but one dramatic event after the other, one bully after another.

It was the peak of summer, and temperatures were sweltering between 118 and 120 degrees that day. She was miserable.

She wondered why it was so difficult for her to work a job without the hassle of being badgered or be sabotaged. All she ever wanted to do was take care of herself and Lauren. She never asked anyone to take care of her. Even though she displayed strength and she had willpower, she was disillusioned with the thought of *Why*

179

can't we just all get along? She had always been a daydreamer.

Cruel reality was setting in, and there was no more time for dillydallying or dreams of winning the lottery or just having a job in corporate America, one she could actually work without being harassed. She had had enough of bad relationships inside and outside of work. She knew she was a good person. At that moment she just wanted everyone to stop on the freeway and listen. But instead she talked herself into becoming strong, stronger than ever.

She was more determined than ever to not quit after what had happened to her; she could not let Dale win. She was going to hold on no matter what. She was tired of pretending it was alright for people to hurt her and then just tuck her tail and move on, letting them get away with taking things away that were rightfully hers. She was pissed off beyond belief and was going to stick it out at CMT for as long as she had to. They were going to pay for what they were doing and for allowing a psychopath to do what he was doing to her.

She took her attorney's advice and waited for the EEOC to do an investigation and find them guilty. She was counting on them and needed them to intervene as soon as possible, but it was wishful thinking. She got a call from a guy at the EEOC asking her some questions. He let her know it would be months, possibly a year before he would be able to investigate her case. He wanted her to just ask for a "right to sue letter." This meant Kay could sue the company for what they had done, and the EEOC would be off the hook in having to do their duty to investigate. It also meant the man would have one less case in his file.

She spoke to her attorney and several other attorneys, and they told her it would cost her thousands of dollars to sue, unless she were able to wait it out for the EEOC to do their job and investigate. If she could get a letter from the EEOC showing "cause," they would take her case for free.

This put Kay in a tight spot. The only thing she had going for her was the fact that she was able to pay her bills every month by going to a job that entailed harassment. She called the EEOC almost every other day and asked the man to please hurry and help her because things were getting worse at work.

Dale had begun pulling her aside, cornering her and making it clear things were going to get worse the longer she stayed. He would whisper childish things like, "Ha! Ha! Nothing will ever happen to me, bitch! You are ruined!"

It was becoming too much, but somehow she did her best to cope. After months of continual harassment not only from Dale but by all of management, she began failing at her job. Nobody would help her bid anything, and that meant no sales.

* * *

During all this, Lauren was getting ready to go to Penn State. Kay took her vacation days and flew to Pennsylvania to be with Lauren while she got situated in her new surroundings. It was beautiful there, and Lauren seemed quite happy with her roommates. It was a bittersweet time for Kay. She was emotional knowing she was done raising Lauren, who was now an adult with a life of her own.

By the time Kay flew back to Arizona, she knew it was time to leave, but she was not about to quit—at least not until she found another job. In the meantime, she prayed the EEOC would do their job so CMT to would have to pay for what they were doing to her.

She was nervous about returning to work and hated it with a passion. The only person that made it bearable was Maria. She was very supportive of Kay and felt bad about everything she was going through. Maria could see Dale harassing Kay by messing around with her work, and she knew he was obsessed with Kay, but there was nothing she could do. She was smart enough to know that Human Resources and management would drive her out, too, if she were to complain or meddle in any way.

When Kay's plane landed in Arizona, she had a headache. She got her luggage and headed to the parking garage. As she approached her car, she went into shock. There was Dale standing by her car. He had somehow found out Kay's itinerary and knew when she would be landing in Phoenix. He had followed her to the airport and watched her park her car before taking off to Pennsylvania. She screamed and started running, and he yelled out "Welcome back!"

She ran into the airport to get security. They went out to check, but there was no trace of him. Dale had somehow dodged security in the parking garage. She was petrified and called the police. She immediately got a restraining order on him, but she had no real proof that he had done anything to her. It would be her word against his. All of the harassment was underhanded, planned, and manipulated to make it look like she was crazy.

The next day when she returned to work, Human Resources called her into Mike's office. They sat her down and told her she would no longer be working for them.

Kay was in shock and yelled out, "Why? You can't do this to me! I have a restraining order against Dale! He followed me to the airport yesterday! What is going on? I am the one being harassed here, so why won't you listen to me? He is sick and is going to do something very bad because you won't do anything to him!" This time she was smart about it. She had bought a mini-recorder and was able to record everything. When they asked her if she could prove he was at the airport, she hesitated and answered "No," in utter disgust.

They continued talking to her as if they had heard nothing. They told her that her numbers were not up to par and that she was being fired for not meeting her quota. Kay knew that was lie, but Dale had fixed the numbers to look as though she wasn't doing her job. They also let her

182

know that other employees in other locations, such as California and Denver, were being let go, due to not meeting their numbers. They knew exactly how to cover their collective corporate asses.

Kay was mortified. She could not believe she was being fired, and all she could do was think about calling her attorney. When they escorted her out of the building with her measly last paycheck, she was completely embarrassed. She immediately got into her car and called her attorney.

He asked her what reason they had for firing her, and she told him the excuse they had given her and let him know it wasn't true. He asked her how difficult would it be to prove that. Kay told him she wasn't sure if she could because Dale had botched the numbers in his favor. Once he heard that, he told her there was nothing he could do for her—that she had the restraining order and would have to wait for the EEOC to finish their investigation, and hopefully they could sort out the truth. Then he told her to move on with her life.

Move on with my life? She thought. *Dale is stalking me, and who knows what he will do next?*

She called Maria and told her what had happened. Maria told her Dale had sent out an email to the entire company telling everyone that Kay was fired for not meeting her quota. Kay screamed out, "What? Oh my God! That has to be against the law!" She told Maria she would call her back, and she called her attorney to tell him what she had just heard.

He told her it was completely legal as long as he was in control and had the paperwork to back up his allegations. Once again, it would be up to the EEOC to investigate and come up with a ruling.

She pulled over to the side of the road and called Maria back, and they decided to meet up at a restaurant. Kay cried as Maria tried to comfort her. Maria let her know that when and if the EEOC ever did call her, she would tell them what she witnessed.

183

But Kay knew it was too late. She had to leave Arizona, as quickly as possible. She did not know what that son of a bitch would do next. Maria agreed. She knew Kay had a difficult past few years living there, and she wanted to see her happy. She really liked Kay, and they had become more than co-workers. They had become friends.

* * *

Kay was turning forty in four days, and it was horrible. She had little money and did not know where to go. She called her parents, and Mark told her to sell everything she could and load up what she had left into the U-Haul and to drive to Utah. She wanted to die at the thought of going back to Utah, but she had no choice.

Within three days, the internet had helped her unload many of her things. She felt the pain of a thousand knives cutting through her chest and back, as she loaded the remainder of her belongings into the U-Haul which she had hitched to her car. The next day, she would be turning forty—with no job, no money, and headed to state that she swore she would never live in again.

As she started up Highway 10 and headed out into the desert, she felt like she was ten years old again, leaving Ohio, crying and begging for someone not to take her back to Utah. Once again she had no choice. She was broke from attorneys' fees and paying high rent. She had nothing left except her few belongings, most of which she sold off to move out of Phoenix. She had only her memorabilia, some dishes, and a few odds and ends.

As Kay drove, she could not help but think about all the hell Phoenix had handed her. It had been the hardest five years of her life, as if her past had not already been tough enough. It was too hard to fathom that it was her fortieth birthday and she had nothing but what a little U-Haul held.

Mark had found some brand new apartments in Salt Lake City that were offering two months free rent with an eighteen-month lease, and Kay was relieved she would not have to live with her parents. A brand new apartment was a good thing; she would at least have clean carpet to sleep on. Her parents met her and helped her unload the boxes from the trailer. They gave her an air mattress for her birthday. *Wow,* she thought. *This is exactly what I've always dreamt of for my fortieth.*

"

What a slime ball!" Lauren yelled, hoping nobody heard her. She became filled with anger as she was reading this revelation. So this is why my mother had to return to Utah! No wonder she has been so adamant about fighting this battle!

She heard the voice of the captain come over the intercom, they would be landing in Newark in approximately 45 minutes; she wanted, no, needed to finish what she reading before the plane landed.

20

Back in Utah again and thinking about all that had happened in Phoenix, Kay was paranoid. She was in the same predicament as when she fifteen and witnessed her father kill himself; she was the only person who knew every detail of what had happened, and nobody could help her erase those memories. She was sick and could not sleep—or rather she did not want to sleep for fear of having nightmare after nightmare, first about her father and now about Dale.

She kept in close contact with Maria. Maria felt so bad about what had happened, and she filled Kay in about the aftermath in the office. She let Kay know daily that everyone knew Dale was a scum bag. She also assured Kay that a lot of people knew she was used and made an example of, but if anyone complained, they would be pushed out of their job. They sent an email as soon as Kay left the office telling everyone she was fired. That email was meant to serve as a warning.

Kay took some comfort in knowing that everyone knew the truth, but it did not change the fact that she was jobless and had only a short time before the little she had would run out. Kay mustered up as much energy as possible to find work, and within two weeks, she had landed a decent-paying job. She was on her way to rebuilding her life once again, but this time was different; she had never lost everything all at once before. This time, she wasn't going to waste her time or energy daydreaming. She was going to do her best to stay in reality and make her life a peaceful one. Still, though, she couldn't help worrying that somehow, Dale would find her and ruin her life at her new job.

As she worked her new sales job, this time selling elevator services, she was once again in a male-dominated industry and treated differently than men, but she did not care. As long as nobody pinned her into corners and stalked her, she would be fine. All that mattered to her was making money in order to rebuild her life...again.

* * *

Her new life included meeting new friends. The apartment building she lived in housed many singles who were consistently on the go. She made friends with a couple who lived next door, and they invited Kay to dinner a couple times a week. Kay felt safe with them, because they had taken her in and were so much fun, not to mention they had a lot of acquaintances of their own.

One night, they invited Kay to join them for a Jazz game. She agreed, having not been to a Jazz game since before she moved to California and excited about the chance to go again. They had great seats on the eleventh row, but while Kay was enjoying the game, watching the action on the court, someone else was watching her.

Kay left her seat to go get a drink and some popcorn. While standing in line waiting for her turn to order, she was surprised by a tap on the shoulder. It took her only a second to recognize the face she was looking at. *Sean*! In somewhat of a state of shock, she gave him a hug. The last she had heard, Sean was married and had two children of his own. She couldn't believe he was standing right next to her at that concession stand. He had seen her walk in and was seated several rows behind her along with his date. He'd been waiting for her to get up so he could follow her.

Sean asked her for her number and told her he was divorced. "I am here with someone but it's nothing serious," he claimed. "I can't wait to get together and catch up with you."

As they talked and gazed into each other's eyes, there was an undeniable spark—one she hadn't felt in what seemed to be forever. Kay was in disbelief. She never thought she would see Sean again, and she was convinced that even if she did bump into him, he'd still be happily married to someone else.

* * *

The next day, just as he promised, Sean called her, and they planned to meet the following evening for dinner at a little Italian restaurant downtown. Kay was overwhelmed. She had lived so many different lives since she had seen Sean last, and he had lived just one regular married one in Utah and married...or so she thought.

They talked for hours, like teenagers again, both of them with butterflies dancing in their stomachs. Sean became teary eyed when he realized what a hard life Kay had lived since he had last seen her in the hospital room after giving birth to Lauren. He told her he had always loved her and never forgot about her. He had learned that she moved to California and admitted he felt a bit sad knowing that he would no longer be able to keep tabs on her whereabouts after she left. He had so many regrets when it came to her. She was his first love, and hearing her painful past made it all the more difficult.

In the meantime, Sean had lived a life of his own. He had become a successful businessman and owned several welding companies. When he discovered his wife cheating on him several years prior, he promptly divorced her and decided to distance himself from the Mormon Church. He told Kay he'd been playing the field and dated a lot of woman during the past two years. But all of that was about to change. He had found his first love again, single as she was, and he wanted so badly to take care of her after hearing about her long, painful journey through the past two decades.

Five hours later, without even realizing they'd been talking that long, Kay and Sean were asked to leave because the restaurant owners wanted to close up shop for the day.

Kay wondered if Sean really was into her again or if he just wanted to reminisce about his past, but she realized the latter was true when he walked her to her car, grabbed her by the arms, and kissed her so hard and long she wanted to pass out. When Sean looked into her eyes and told her he didn't want to let go, she assured him she felt the same way and hoped he really meant what he was saying. After years of being played by dozens of men, Kay needed that reassurance.

After a few more long, passionate kisses and gazes that spoke volumes of unspoken apologies and desires, Sean asked her to see him the next evening. "I'll make you dinner at my place," he offered.

And of course Kay agreed.

* * *

Kay was stunned to see how well Sean had done for himself. He owned ten acres and a beautiful brand new home in the center of it all. She loved his place right away and felt comfortable as soon as she set foot outside the car. The thought did occur to her, *How many women have felt the same way walking through these doors?* But what Kay did not yet realize was that Sean was 100 percent into her; nobody—not his ex-wife and none of the women he'd been with since—had ever or could ever trump the love he had for her.

They spent that evening together and, just as Kay had hoped, he made love to her. Amazingly, it was better than their first time at age seventeen. Cliché as it might sound, she was falling in love with him all over again, but part of her was still petrified. *What if he is just playing me?* continually ran through her mind.

Sean did not want her to leave the next morning. He made her breakfast and asked what she was doing that day. He had promised himself while holding her in his arms the night before that from that day on, Kay would be in his life forever. She would be his.

Kay, however, had a hard time believing anything so wonderful could really last long. After all, she had nothing in the past to go on but bouts of bad luck. As she watched Sean flipping the bacon over in his skillet, she couldn't help but hope that this time it would last. She couldn't believe she was in Utah and actually was enjoying herself.

* * *

Kay continued speaking to Maria, almost daily. Maria was ecstatic that Kay had found something (or someone) that brought her happiness. In the midst of their daily discussions of Sean and her newfound relationship with him, Maria always filled Kay in on what was happening with Dale. "He's set his sights on another woman," she finally blurted out. "Her name's Kris, and he has a full-on obsession with her. Poor girl's only twenty-three years old, too naïve to even realize she's being sexually harassed. She has no idea how to say no to that monster." She went on to tell Kay that Dale rode daily in Kris's car to every appointment she had. Maria could not believe how blatant he was about his obsession, once again putting a female co-worker in an uncomfortable position and getting away with it.

Kay was disgusted but it was admittedly some kind of relief to know that the scumbag was far away in Arizona, fixated on some other unfortunate soul, and that kept him from following her around. Kay continually warned Maria that Dale was a psychopath and worried about what he would do if Kris finally broke down and told him to get lost. Kay also knew that if Kris did not tell him to stop or pull away, something bad would happen.

191

The calls from Maria started to become more frequent as Dale's obsession with Kris started to become more and more obvious to everyone. Maria told Kay her name came up on occasion, followed by, "Yeah, I guess she was right about Dale."

* * *

Weeks turned into months, and it wasn't long before the holidays were approaching. Kay and Sean were together almost every evening, and one night he asked her to move in with him. Part of her wanted to but she had just furnished her apartment and was getting back some self-esteem that came from rebuilding her life again; she didn't want to move too quickly into anything that could potentially backfire or stand in the way of her dream of moving back to California someday.

Kay did not know how to handle being in a long-term loving relationship with anything but a beautiful view. Her life had been filled with disappointment when it came to men and trusting that someone could truly love her was not something she could comprehend. As much as she wanted to believe Sean loved her, she was no longer the naïve girl he knew as a teenager.

* * *

Kay was involved in her job and still seeking justice for what had happened in Arizona. She wanted and needed some closure in regard to the situation in Arizona. She wanted to prevent someone else from going through what she had to go through, but it was happening again and she wanted CMT to pay for what they were allowing Dale to do. Kay called the EEOC once a week and begged the man working on her case to investigate. She also told them she feared that there was another woman being harassed. It was always the same story; he had many other cases and did not know when he would get around to hers.

Kay was frustrated with the system and could not believe that corporate America and even the EEOC were of no help to her. She was starting to believe that the EEOC was there to protect the companies and not the employees. Just like Human Resources, it was all a racket. The injustice made her sick. She had witnessed so much of it in her life, and it was intolerable for her to just sit back and let the situation go on. She was determined to put pressure on the EEOC to do their job.

Maria told Kay story after story about how Dale followed Kris around. She said Kris was the only employee he paid attention to and that everyone in the office was talking about it. Maria was sick of watching this man do what he did to Kay all over again. All the while CMT looked the other way and did nothing to stop the pervert or get rid of him.

It would be months or even years before the EEOC would do their job. In the meantime, CMT allowed Dale to creep around, sniffing after Kris like a dog in heat. It was a crime, but nobody was doing anything to make it stop.

It was several weeks before Christmas, and Kay was doing great at her new job and she was falling more in love with Sean every day, things were going along well until she received a call from Maria. Maria let Kay know that Kris and Dale had gotten into a big argument in the middle of the office and that Kris told him in no uncertain terms to stay away from her, right in front of everyone.

Kay screamed with joy, "Finally! Finally! Somebody will have to fix things now. He's not going to get away with it!"

Maria explained to Kay in detail the entire fight. What stuck out to Kay the most was the way Maria described Dale's eyes when Kris was yelling at him. She told her they were red, and he was staring at Kris like he wanted to kill her; as his eyes became redder as did his balding head. Kay was concerned, because she knew the monster would resort to anything to get back at someone that threatened his already filthy reputation.

He had followed Kay around for months, including to her home and God-only-knew where else, all thanks to CMT. She wondered what would they give him permission to do next, and she was worried about Kris and also her friend Maria. Kay told Maria she should take some time off to stay away from the office. She had a bad feeling and hated Maria being around that man. He was an unstable son of a bitch, and the holidays were the perfect time for a lonely psychopath to go all-out crazy. Kay felt comfort knowing she was far away from him, but she couldn't help being concerned for Maria.

* * *

Christmas came and Sean asked Kay to move in with him again and she once again turned him down she let him know she needed time. He had a hard time understanding, most women would have jumped at the idea of moving in with Sean, he couldn't understand how deep her fears ran or what demons her past really held.

It was Friday, New Year's Eve day, and Maria and Kay had not spoken since right before Christmas. She sent Maria a text wishing her "Happy New Year" and received a response of "Who is this?"

Kay called Maria's phone, but instead of Maria's voice, a man answered. It was Daniel, Maria's fiancé. He said, "Who is this?"

Kay told him who she was.

Daniel then began to tell Kay that Maria was in intensive care.

She exclaimed "What happened?"

"Maria's boss came into work and opened fire in the office. A woman named Kris was killed and so were several others. Maria and Mike, the General Manager, were wounded."

Kay screamed, "Oh my God!"

"Maria was shot in the back while sitting at her desk. We are not sure...they...they don't know if she will walk again." His voice cracked.

Kay started crying. Daniel continued on, Kay immediately ran to her computer and went to read about the "Workplace Shooting Phoenix Arizona." The article said Dale Shrake, a manager at CMT, opened fire, killing two people and wounding several others. He was on the run, and police were looking for him.

Kay panicked and began yelling, "Oh my God! I knew it! I told Maria to take off work! What a son of a bitch! I want to kill him! I want to kill him!"

Daniel stopped her and told Kay she needed to call the police. He knew about her and that she had a lawsuit with CMT all because of Dale.
Kay got off the phone and called the Phoenix police, as well as the Salt Lake City police department. Within fifteen minutes an officer was at her door. They began searching for his car, as well as checking all Salt Lake City flights that he could be on. Kay was petrified! Maria was in so much pain but she still continued to call Kay because she feared Kay was going to be killed. She had just witnessed the madman kill and she knew Kay would be on his hit list.

Kay felt helpless with the restraining order in place. She wanted to fly to Phoenix and be there for Maria because she felt guilty. She thought she had made it clear enough to everyone that Dale was a madman, but she thought maybe she hadn't screamed or yelled enough to get help. Still, she didn't know what more she could have done. She would spend the next twenty-four hours trying to decide whether or not to go.

Before she left for Phoenix, Kay headed out to get something to eat. She hated leaving her apartment, she was in fear, but knew she couldn't stay locked up forever. She drove to buy a sandwich and drink. When she returned home, she got out of her car and started walking back to her apartment. Suddenly, she heard a sound that had haunted her for years: the piercing sound of a gunshot! She screamed and started running. She did not know what direction the shot had come from, but she knew it was close. She immediately dove into some bushes. Her blood was rushing through her veins, giving her an instant headache. She did her best not to move or breathe. She heard footsteps coming near her, and as they came closer, she rolled up into a ball.

She heard men struggling as another gunshot went off, and she screamed. People began running over to the scene. It was dark, and she finally jumped out of the bushes in pure rage, ready to attack, but she looked up and saw a man standing on Dale's back as he struggled to get away. More men jumped in to help the stranger contain Dale. She ran over to Dale as he lay on the ground with his ugly face shoved into the pavement. She began kicking his face and head with her boots. She was raging mad, and people were trying to stop her, but she continued to kick him with her heel, hoping he would die. The men that were holding him down were telling Kay to stop. Finally, another man pulled Kay to the ground, and she went into shock and could not move.

Within minutes, police officers and an ambulance arrived at the scene. The men that brought down Dale had no idea Kay was his target. All they knew was that there was a madman with a gun shooting in the apartment complex.

Kay's body had broken down. She was traumatized, and her post-traumatic stress disorder had set in when she heard the gunshot. She was admitted to the hospital for evaluation and stayed in the hospital for several days, until she was unable to function.

When she was told Dale had died on the way to the hospital, she was relieved. He had caused enough pain, and it was good to know the world was finally rid of someone who was just pure garbage.

* * *

There was enough mess to clean up, and while Kay was being nursed back to health, she had been contacted by her attorney. She let him know she would be seeking other counsel—somebody who was willing to take her case to trial and not wait for the EEOC, who were obviously dragging their feet. She was pissed off and ready to take down CMT and make sure every employee in America understood that Human Resources and the EEOC were not there to help anyone except the companies or corporations that were being accused of breaking the law.

Lauren was exhausted and took a deep breathe while trying to hold back more tears.

She felt overwhelmed with guilt. She always thought her mother was the one stressing her out and now she realized she had put her mother through more hell than she ever deserved.

As she laid her head back and looked out the window, she felt herself letting the resentment towards her mother fade away. She knew now that all of her mother's decisions to move over the years had been intended to find security and possibly love.

Instead her mother kept finding more unjustified pain.

21

Sean had become Kay's rock, and more than anything, he wanted to protect her. He immediately hired men to pack up her apartment and put things in storage, and he moved her in with him.

Kay was unable to return to her new job after what had happened, for she was far too traumatized. CMT made several attempts to settle out of court. One offer was two million, but Kay had found an attorney named Robert Ross who was one hundred percent in line with what Kay was looking for. He was a hot-shot trial attorney that normally represented large corporations, and he was willing to take on her case. Kay wanted someone like him, someone who knew the other side's tactics and was willing to fight dirty. He agreed with Kay that the case was not only about money but also about justice. She was completely ready to bring the injustice out of the closet. Her pain, Maria's pain, CMT, and their sorry plan to rid people with legitimate complaints: all of it was over. She knew it would be a long, drawn-out fight that would probably take well over a year, but she did not care.

Kay wanted to take out a loan to support herself until the trial was over, but Sean insisted on looking after her. He had the means to meet her every need, and even though she hated not being able to support herself, she allowed him to provide for her. She did, however, make it clear that she would pay him back every cent, and she had every intention of doing so.

Kay spent all her time and energy preparing for the fight of her life. She wanted all employees in the country to know that Human Resources and the EEOC were simply there to help corporations cover up their unethical practices, not to help them. For Kay, it was going to be the trial of her life, and she hoped it would not only provide closure to this injustice, bullying, and harassment, but that it would also help heal all the other bullying she had endured throughout her life.

* * *

CMT became desperate and contacted Robert Ross to make one last attempt at settlement. The EEOC was now attacking CMT, wanting to find out exactly what had gone wrong so they didn't get thrown under the bus in the process. The EEOC investigator Kay had been begging to help her had his own alibi because, like every employee at the EEOC, he had too many cases and could not handle the workload. It was all a cover, as nobody wanted to do their job, but nobody wanted to lose their job either.

CMT hoped to stave off a long, harsh trial that would give them too much bad press. The final offer for settlement was five million. Kay told Robert to tell them to go to hell and because it wasn't all about money and that she would see them in court. The attorneys representing CMT did their best to persuade Robert, but no offer would be enough. She wanted to go to trial.

Several of the others that were injured by Dale took settlements. Maria had let her know that she would stand by her no matter what, and she also turned down the settlement attempts. Maria was in a wheelchair, going through physical therapy

Kay was in a different kind of therapy altogether, which was psychological. She had been traumatized beyond belief from the events that had taken place over the past year involving Dale and CMT. It was a difficult journey for Kay, as she spent hours in therapy with a doctor named Sam Henderson. He was helping her face her demons. She was reluctant at first and told him she didn't feel comfortable talking about her past. The pain was too deep and the secrets too many to count. He recommended that Kay write, even if in third person. He knew if she were able to get it down on paper it would

200

help her deal with her post- traumatic-stress- disorder and help him treat her.

It was not easy, but once Kay started getting the words on paper, things just flowed. She couldn't stop writing, getting all of the pain from her past out on paper was therapy. Her notebook had become her lifeline. She was still having nightmares, but as each week passed, Dr. Henderson learned more about her, he was able to help Kay understand her feelings and emotions and how deal with them.

* * *

CMT had no idea that the woman they fired for warning them that Dale was a madman had enough experience to know what she was talking about. They were in for the fight of their life.

Kay and her attorney had gathered a team of the best attorney's in the state of Arizona. She felt so lucky to have Sean and to have the much-needed time to spend healing.

Lauren had quit school and started practicing in order to go pro. Even though Kay was not happy about Lauren's decision, she understood. Lauren let her mother know she would be going to Scotland and playing in the European Tournament and hoped Kay would be able to come and watch. They had started to communicate and it was because Lauren was growing up. It was a dream for Kay to be able to spend quality time with her daughter and to see Scotland.

Dr. Sam Henderson went through evaluating Kay and preparing her to testify and heal. Each week Dr. Henderson would read over Kay's writings and they would discuss her history. It was the first time Kay actually was able to acknowledge her troubled past. His testimony would be crucial for the defense in rebuttal for what had taken place before CMT let her go. They were going to say they had no reason to believe anything Kay had to say. Even though Kay had twenty emails begging them to help her and transfer her away from Dale because she was afraid of him. They had their own story and all the money in the world to defend themselves. It was going to be up to the jury to see the mound of evidence for what it was and listen to the testimony of Dr. Henderson, Maria and several others. Their testimony would hopefully help the Jury see the truth.

     Dr. Henderson agreed it would be a good idea for Kay to get away before the trial and go with Lauren to Scotland. He knew they had needed some time alone to work on their own mother/daughter relationship.

Holy shit! My mom turned down five million dollars!

She continued to ponder her mother's past. It made sense that she wanted to fight back, but five million dollars was an unbelievable amount of money to turn down. Lauren had often asked her mother, "How much do you think you will get?"

Kay always responded, "It does not matter, just as long as the truth comes out."

After Lauren finished reading her mother's last entry, she tucked the notebook back inside of the file folder. As the plane descended into Newark, Lauren realized she wanted to be at the trial. She was going to meet with the editor of Golf Digest but pass on playing in the tournament. She wanted to surprise her mother by showing up in Phoenix. It was time for her to make amends with the woman she thought she knew.

22

Kay arrived in Phoenix and met with Ross and his team. They were ready and could not wait to get started. Ross was cautiously optimistic. For him, it was not only about the notoriety; he also wanted the money.

If they won the case would set a precedent that all corporations, as well as the EEOC, would be held accountable if they ignored sexual harassment claims.

Kay was nervous the night before the trial. She had a hard time sleeping and woke to the sound of the infamous gunshot. She knew it was only due to the tremendous amount of stress she had undergone. She missed Sean and knew he was planning on arriving in Phoenix that evening, and she hoped his presence would help ease her anxiety. She could have taken the five million and been living her life along the coast in Carmel. Instead, she gambled it all to make a point. It was a crap shoot, and she was rolling the dice. But she knew part of her gamble included Sean. Her dream of living near the ocean was fading as her love for him grew.

* * *

As Kay and her attorneys walked up to the courthouse the next day, there was a bevy of media everywhere. They were yelling out questions: "Do you really think you can win? Is it true you turned down millions in settlement money?"

Kay had been briefed and knew what she was walking into. The fight was on.

Day one was difficult and long, with many hours of testimony and cross examination. The first day was mainly managers of CMT who had witnessed specific things that took place before Kay was let go.

Kay was exhausted and knew that the next few days would include hers and Maria's testimony. She was happy the first day was over, and when she got back to the hotel, Sean was waiting for her in her room. It felt so good to have him wrap his arms around her. Kay realized Sean stepping back into her life at that time couldn't have been more perfect.

They went to dinner with Mark and Suzanne, and Kay was shocked to see Lauren. She couldn't believe her daughter had come to Phoenix to stand by her side. "Didn't you have a tournament?"

"Yes, but I changed my mind. I wanted to be here for you. I love you, Mom, and I am so sorry for all the pain I've caused you through the years."

Kay was puzzled until Lauren handed her the folder. Kay had wondered if Lauren had read what she had mistakenly left behind, but she had been so busy preparing for court that she had totally forgotten about the file. Kay asked her if she had read it, and Lauren just broke down in tears and hugged her.

Mark and Suzanne were confused and couldn't understand why their granddaughter was behaving so strangely.

Lauren looked at them all and said, "I know everything now!"

Mark replied, "Everything?"

"Yes, Grandpa. I know about Mom's past...and Grandpa Whitley."

Everyone fell silent, and Kay realized that the only person who did not know the full story was Sean. Kay began to explain that it was all very complicated and that they would discuss it later.

After dinner, Kay and Lauren went to Lauren's room, where they spent several hours crying and recapping the past. Kay let Lauren know that her leaving the file behind was not on purpose and that she had intended to tell her everything "one day." She said the information she had written down was really for Dr. Henderson to help her in therapy and it was not intended for anyone else's eyes.

Kay then spent the rest of the evening with Sean and told him about her past. He was in disbelief; he had met as teenager's less than a year after her father's murder-suicide and could not believe she had kept it a secret for all those years. Everyone knew the truth now, and Kay felt a sense of relief.

Sean was only able to stay for a couple of days, though he sincerely wished he could stay with her through the whole trial; he had to be back in Salt Lake City because he was in the middle of an important acquisition. Sean knew that when the trial was over and she returned to Utah he was going to ask her to marry him. Kay had no idea that a proposal was on the horizon.

* * *

The next day, Kay took the stand. As she told her story, she noticed that several jurors looked annoyed. Kay wasn't sure if it was because of her or because they were bothered by CMT and their irresponsibility.

The following day, Maria took stand she was now using a cane to get around. She had made great strides in physical therapy over the past year. It did not take long for her testimony and cross examination. CMT knew they had lost, but they wanted to find out just how much it was going to cost them.

* * *

It took the jury three days to deliberate, and it was a nerve-racking wait. Kay and her attorney had expected it to be only hours. Mark, Suzanne, and Lauren were still in Phoenix awaiting the verdict. While they sat waiting for the judge and jury to appear, Kay became nauseous as many possible outcomes raced through her head. Lauren sat holding Kay's hand. Kay turned around to see Maria, and they smiled at each other. Kay adored Maria and knew they were about to find out if their fight and holding their ground was worth it.

Once the jury and judge had filed in and were situated, the judge asked the jurors if they had reached a verdict.

"Yes, Your Honor, we have," said the jury foreman.

"Please read the verdict."

"We find the defendant guilty on all charges. We award the plaintiff, Kay Kelley ten million dollars and plaintiff Maria Martinez fifteen million."

There was an eruption from the courtroom, and the judge had to slam his gavel and order silence.

"We also want to award all attorneys' fees and medical expenses derived from this incident for each plaintiff. Furthermore, we demand that the defendant cease from any further discrimination and all harassment. We also ask that the EEOC be investigated and held liable for their part and their negligence in this horrific crime."

There was a loud roar from the courtroom, and the judge once again had to order silence.

Kay looked over at Maria, who had tears in her eyes, and the friends embraced in a hug. They had done it, and the hell and torment was finally over. Best of all, Kay had held her own and made it happen! CMT had to pay, and they only had thirty days to make the money available to Kay and Maria.

Kay had not only found justice for what CMT put her through, but from the bullying she had endured from her father and other family members, including Jesse. More importantly, she felt free and empowered, especially from the injustice and helplessness she felt about Lauren's rape. Someone had finally heard and believed her, and she could put all the loss and heartbreak from all the losers and bullies and psychopaths in her life behind her. The pain she had endured would hopefully prevent others from going through what her and her co-workers were subjected to. Kay and Lauren walked out of the courthouse hand and hand, champions reveling in an important moral and ethical victory.

After watching Kay and her attorney answer reporters' questions, Lauren took her mother's arm and walked her down to the car, which Mark had parked in front of the courthouse. They got into the back seat, and Kay hugged Lauren while squealing with joy and relief. Kay comfortably leaned into Lauren, and Lauren pulled out a gift from behind the seat and handed it to Kay. It was enough that Lauren had been thoughtful enough to come to Phoenix, so the gift was just an added surprise. She immediately opened it and saw that it was a draft of an article about Lauren that would be released in the November's *Golf Digest*. The article read: "Lauren Kelley: Young Golfer Takes the Golf World by Storm. Kelley tells her story and dedicates this article to her mother Kay...To my mother, the epitome of strength and persistence. Her resilience has set an example that has kept me on course and given me the drive to focus on my dreams."

As Mark drove them all away from the courthouse and headed to the airport, Kay's tear dropped onto the page she was reading. For a moment, she felt innocent and young again, as if nothing bad had ever happened—her painful childhood, the horrible night with her father and Gina, Jesse, Lauren's rape and the pain caused by a corporation hell bent on covering up the dark truth. It was all just gone, swallowed up by a peace and calmness that washed over Kay, a feeling she had only felt as a very young child, lying in the grass, watching the planes overhead, drawing lines in the Ohio sky.

Denise Landry worked as a Sales Representative for over fifteen years. She now resides in Salt Lake City and is self-employed working as an Employment Recruiter and enjoys writing in her spare time.

Her only child Kelsey currently attends Weber State University and is receiving a full ride golf scholarship; she hopes to turn Professional after graduating in 2013.

www.forgottenpages.com

"Cover Illustrated by Farah Stephens"

www.farahslife.com

www.ingramcontent.com/pod-product-compliance
Lightning Source LLC
Chambersburg PA
CBHW050932120626
46552CB00001B/171